TREIF MAGIC

JOHN BALTISBERGER

To everyone who donated in support
of my daughter Aziza, these are the acts
of loving kindness that will heal the world.

⅁ROLOGUE

IT **WAS EARLY** Sunday morning, the sun hadn't even considered rising yet, and anyone with any sense would continue to call it night, even though the hour hand had passed midnight. I did not want to be awake. Sleep troubled the corners of my eyes as I stared groggily into the mirror. The face on the other side was not mine; a man about a decade or two older than me watched back, his skin apparently soaked with sweat, pale and clammy. I say apparently because this man had no body, no skin, only the appearance of it. I leaned over to see my reflection beside the man in the mirror: sunken dark eyes, scruffy short beard, and unkempt brown hair. Mine was certainly not the face that would inspire trust in the family that had invited me in, let alone the dybbuk I was now supposed to exorcise.

I had left my small apartment as soon as I saw those three stars in the sky signifying the end of Shabbot[1], sped through a mikvah[2]—a natural spring for cleansing—and then drove for ten hours straight to Memphis as quickly as possible. Under most circumstances, a single dybbuk[3] wouldn't be enough

---

1 Jewish day of rest, Friday sundown to Saturday sundown.

2 Ritual purification bath

to cause this much of a rush, but the middle-aged and unsettling man had taken up residence in the bathroom of a teenage girl. Cases which involve children always get the rabbinic rush. I may have even tried arguing, but teenagers are extra susceptible to possession; I think it has something to do with their potential for experience. I turned my pale green eyes back to the watery brown eyes of the dybbuk and attempted to give a smile that wasn't weary or irritated. This smile has never been my strong point, and the thing in the mirror looked like it was going to begin crying. Terrific.

"At least you're you," I muttered. Dybbukim[4], while not fun or always easy, are generally not a violent affair; unlike some of the things I get sent after, dybbukim could be reasonable. "I'm just going to get a few things from my bag," I offered, as much for the dybbuk's sake as for the family waiting outside the bathroom. "Then I'll be back, and you and I can talk, okay?" I stepped out of the bathroom and rubbed my eyes. When I opened them again, I saw three people gazing at me with a mix of disbelief and fear. I tried my best to give an apologetic, closed-mouth smile—which, as previously stated, is not my strong point—and moved to my bag.

"What are you getting?" His voice had more than a bit of a challenge. I glanced up while opening the large duffel bag, and reminded myself that these people were facing something that they likely didn't even believe existed before a day or so ago.

---

3   A ghost

4   The plural for ghost.

2

"Incense, made from Thai holy basil. A shofar[5], gallon of spring water and some salt."

"Why are you offering the ghost a meal?" This from the daughter; she had that strange way of talking that so many teens seem to use, pretending to be bored and disinterested when they were actually far more curious than is healthy.

"Not a meal, just something to soothe and relax . . . everyone." I moved back into the bathroom, arms cradling all of my items, hoping the doorway would serve as a barrier to any more of their questions; of course, it never did. After a moment I looked back.

"Rabbi Kaplan, I feel like there has to be some other explanation for what's going on . . . the idea that there's some sort of ghost living in my daughter's mirror or that my synagogue has some exorcist on payroll is ludicrous; I used to work on the board, and I think I would have noticed that line in our budget. I mean, I didn't think we even did that sort of thing."

"Just Ze'ev[6], please; I'm not a rabbi, rebbe[7], or anything like that—I'm just a man who happens to have some specialized training." Out of my bag, I pulled a gallon of spring water and the other items I had mentioned, setting them on the ground around me. "As far as what Jews believe, well, over the ages we have considered a lot of things; for instance, are you familiar with the ordeal of bitter water?" Mr. Cohen shook his head, staring at me blankly.

"It's a potion—or a ritual that involved a potion—

---

5   A curved ram's horn, blown as an instrument.

6   Ze'ev or Zev is a Hebrew name meaning "Wolf"

7   A Jewish spiritual leader, similar to a rabbi.

extrapolated from the book of numbers, mentioned in the Mishna[8] and then ratified and explained in the Talmud. The ordeal of bitter water is when a woman is suspected of being unfaithful, but there are no witnesses to the crime. A special potion was made in a special type of jug, and the woman had to drink it; now this was a special kind of potion." I glanced up. The entire family was staring at me, looking perplexed. It was the young girl, Sandy, who spoke first.

It was the young girl, Sandy, who spoke first. "We made potions? What did this potion do?" Curious girl; I liked her—she reminded me of myself, always questioning, seeking knowledge without actually being smart enough to know when learning wasn't the best thing to attain.

"Not only did we make potions, but we also cursed them. This cursed potion, when drunk by an adulteress, killed her. If she was innocent, not so much." I shrugged a little. "Of course, if someone were to bribe the one making the potion to put some poison in . . . " I shrugged again. Trying to divorce faith from politics was impossible, even when it came to the occult. "So when you ask if we believe in ghosts, and exorcisms . . . Sometimes we leave beliefs aside when we as a faith outgrow them, and sometimes they just become quieter. For instance, if I refused to believe in ghosts, who would be here now, helping you with your dybbuk?" I smiled a little to try to regain my patience. "If you could all move into the living room and pray for me, that would be most helpful."

Slowly, they complied. I doubted they would pray with much fervor, but any prayers would help, and the

---

8   The oral Torah

privacy of them leaving would be incredibly beneficial to my state of mind. I breathed out, and then gave what felt like a much more genuine smile in the direction of the mirror before stopping the sink and pouring in the spring water and salt. I would have preferred a natural spring or creek water, but I doubted the Cohens had a natural spring running through any of their rooms. The salt was for me, really; it reminded me of the ocean and helped put me at ease. I placed a ceramic ashtray on the edge of the sink and lit the incense I had brought with me in the center, watching the slow, lazy smoke rise before I turned off the light and finally lit two candles. It now looked appropriately spooky, or romantic.

"Atah gabor l'Olam Adonai, v'neshama shenatata bi, t' hora he." I began the intonation quietly; it meant: "Yours is the only strength there is, and the soul you have given me is pure." No matter what assignment I'm dealing with—from something as innocuous as a harmless dybbuk, or as dangerous as sheydim[9] gone mad—I start with that small mantra, used to focus my mind on the task at hand. It also serves to remind me that no matter what I do, no matter what my adversary does, all power stems from the Ein Sof[10], from G-d.

My teacher, Rabbi Gershon, had always taught me that exorcisms were a form of healing. You were healing the possessed, sure; but you were also healing the spirit, bringing it back in line with how the world should be, so that it could move on and claim its place

---

9 A Jewish faerie or Demon, said to be half formed at the beginning of the first Shabbot.

10 Infinite Nothingness, a term for G-d

in the world to come. Like in AA, sometimes people didn't want healing. Reb[11] Gershon taught me that, too—in between sips of whiskey.

This seemed to be going fine; I whispered Hebrew psalms softly as I watched the ghostly face in the mirror. It appeared worried, but not angry. When I finished the psalms, I sat on the toilet facing the mirror and met the spirit's eyes. It was essential to be comforting, which was discomforting for me. Give me some bloodsucking sheydim or mischievous spirit any day. I am not a counselor, I'm not a therapist; it's one of the many reasons I dropped out of rabbinical school. But it was, as I already said, part of the job.

"Okay, you're here, and you shouldn't be right?" No answer. "And because you're here, the young woman in the other room is scared, her family is scared—that probably isn't what you want, right? So, talk to me; tell me why it is you are here." I closed my eyes. I was exhausted, as usual, but I was also tired; something about this place just pulled all the energy out of me.

Without opening my eyes, I reached out and pressed my hand against the mirror. It was cool; calming, almost. It felt safer somehow, like whatever was on the other side of this mirror was a better place. Usually when something is wrong, it happens so slowly—so insidiously—that it takes feeling something right to make you realize that things have gotten twisted. That's one reason acts of kindness are so valuable—not in and of themselves, but because they point out how fucked the acts of violence are. Something was off here. "Tell me why you are here."

When the dead speak without a body, it is awful; like

---

11 A short term for Rebbe or Rabbi

something slithering through the muck and slime, slipping out of a marsh into a bathtub that should be clean. It only added to the wrongness I was feeling. But what was worse was the word it uttered when it did choose to speak.

"Brought."

Typically speaking to the dead is strictly forbidden; only in the midst of exorcism are those rules relaxed, and with good reason. This isn't the only place, the only world or reality, whatever you want to call it; there are most certainly others, and pulling souls in and out of this one through necromantic rites could easily tear a hole in the walls, opening a doorway big enough for things not properly created to slip through. I raised my eyes to the face in the mirror once more, and it was smiling at me—a malicious smile with teeth that looked like they were growing longer. The dybbuk no longer looked meek or unassuming; it looked hungry, and it was swelling, filling up the space in the mirror.

I was better at this; dropping the charade of the counselor, I could act in defiance of something violent. My fingers moved of their own accord, swiping through the ashes of the incense and then across the face of the mirror, drawing each name quickly and perfectly in Hebrew across the image of the spirit's face and my own:

'BRH BRQY'L ' DWNY'L ZRY'L

"For he will come at you at night, and you will say to him: 'Who are you? Withdraw from humanity and from the children of HaShem.[12]"

---

12 The Name, another term for G-d.

BRKY'L MY'L QDS Y'L MRGY'L

"For your appearance is one of vanity, and your horns are horns of illusion." The dybbuk's face twisted with hate now; mouth open in silent screams, it reached towards the mirror seeking to smudge the angelic names I wrote.

PRW'L PNY'L MRBNY'L MRNYS'L

"You are darkness, not light, wickedness, not righteousness, and these . . . "

SMY'L MNY'L MTN'L HWD HWD

"These are they who stand upon the eighth step, their appearance is as shining amber, they speed their deeds, trembling and fire are in their dwelling place. Their presence is filled with fear, they rule the spirits that wander the earth, and in a place where their name is invoked an evil spirit may not enter." I reached through the mirror, made flimsy by the dybbuk's efforts, and grabbed its throat to pull it through and into my control. It howled and a wild wind whipped through the bathroom.

"The commander of the army, Adonai[13], will bring you down into deepest Sheol[14], the two bronze gates through which no light can enter, and the sun will not shine for you that rises upon the righteous!" The dybbuk was weightless, and I reached up and threw

13 Another name for G-D, used to denote the holy tetragrammaton.

14 A version of the afterlife that is akin to imprisonment.

the thing down at the ground as hard as I could—not that Sheol is literally down or beneath, but the symbols of things are important. With a ghastly hiss, the dybbuk began sinking through the floor, roaring and gnashing its teeth at me the entire time. The language was something other than English, but it was not Hebrew or Spanish either.

I watched until it had sunken out of view and the wind had stopped howling in the bathroom. With one shaking hand, I wiped the ash off the mirror. "Baruch Atah Adonai ha-gomel lechayavim tovos shegemalani tov." I breathed out the prayer as I sat back against the wall and rested my head.

"Mi shegamalcha tov, hu yigmalcha kol tov selah," came the quivering voice of the teenage girl. I cracked one eye open to look at her; she was wide-eyed— freaked out would not be inaccurate. "I thought you said this was going be relaxed."

I couldn't help it; I started laughing, and after a minute she laughed, too.

"They can't all be easy, apparently." I finally rose, gathered my supplies, and after refusing any payment several times I walked out of the front door to my beat-up and elderly Dodge muscle car. I would probably try to find a hotel somewhere along the way—maybe that big dumb pyramid I had passed on my way into Memphis. I needed to rest, I needed to catch my breath; but most importantly, I needed to know what schlump[15] was dabbling in opening doors for the dead.

---

15 Yiddish for a pathetic person.

CHAPTER 1

IT TURNS OUT that the crazy pyramid I had seen coming into Memphis was a hunting and fishing store; they did have a hotel, but the cost of staying there or even eating in the restaurant was far more than my per diem allowed. After being rebuffed by the prices there, I turned to my old standby: La Quinta and fast food. Keeping kosher on the road was never easy, but a local cheese pizza and whiskey and coke never failed me during these out-of-town trips. The room I was staying in was not particularly inviting, but there is something comforting about being in the same room you've been in a thousand times before. These little motels had been a constant throughout my life. They hadn't changed during the nearly thirty years I had been staying in them. First on family road trips across the country to visit family that wasn't crazy enough to live in small nothing towns in the South, and then more and more on business and school trips. I had stayed in some nicer hotels—mostly when I first started traveling for work—but in general I found that they didn't really offer anything more than the motels. They had the same twin beds, the same mini-fridges and wall safes. I had seen the idyllic image of a babbling brook next to an old cottage in the woods over beds in these places countless times. The same eggshell white walls greeted me no matter what door I entered at the end of a long day.

I kicked my legs up on the desk in the corner, taking another slice of pizza and, not for the first time, wondering why I didn't just bite the bullet and move to New York so I could get real pizza. The simple answer, of course, is that they didn't need me in the North at all. They needed me—or at least someone with my particular skill set—down here in the South. We have territories, and since I was used to the heat and schlepping hundreds of miles to get between cities, it just made sense to keep me here. Of course, it didn't help that I rubbed a lot of my superiors the wrong way. You would think that an organization that needs people with such a specialized skill set would be less judgmental. Chewing on the crust, I pulled open my laptop and got started on the paperwork and reporting I would need to do.

Red tape was an amusing part of the job; after all, who was looking at these receipts and reports? My paychecks bore the mark of the Central Conference of American Rabbis. I was technically a member of the clergy; I think that on the paperwork that went through the system, I was listed as a cantor, or prayer leader. I snapped a few pictures of receipts, filled out an expense report, and wrote up a quick report from the exorcism. Because no one had been injured, despite the potentially violent entity, the paperwork was relatively simple and straightforward. It was made a little more difficult by the invocation of angelic names. Ideally, an exorcism should be more of a conversation than a battle. There are plenty of things out there that intend violence, or that simply feed off humankind. Those things aren't usually my problem, unless for some reason they end up specifically targeting Jewish communities. A dybbuk, generally speaking, isn't that sort of issue. More often than not they are simply having trouble letting go of some deep regret. I once spoke to a vegetarian dybbuk who had never had a really good burger, and refused to leave this world without trying one. Of course, there were truly vile spirits that refused to leave because they feared some divine retribution. I much prefer the cases where I get to enjoy a burger.

Then there was the matter of Sandy Cohen. She was a child, no matter what the Bat Mitzvah[16] ceremony said or symbolized, and children who are exposed to the supernatural would never live just mundane lives like everyone else. There was a point in life where you were able to handle things like that and maintain your equilibrium; before that point, though, serious brushes with the supernatural somehow touched the soul. Not a small thing like mischievous creatures hiding your keys, but things like being haunted, or attacked by the inhuman things that creep through the shadows—these things leave an indelible mark upon our psyche. It's a mark that seems to draw the supernatural to us. This was the thing that had driven me into the life I now led. It wasn't a life that I would wish on anyone, but it was one with which I was intimately familiar. I suggested that Sandy Cohen be observed for signs of interest in the paranormal, and if need be, be trained as a

16 Coming of age ceremony for young girls.

counselor or adviser—anything other than an exorcist.

I had just bundled all of the paperwork into a zip file to send off and was getting ready to close the computer when I noticed an email waiting for me— an email from a very familiar address. I grimaced; Nathan Schulman was an old acquaintance, and he had been my Torah teacher in Yeshiva[17] for a while. Then, when I had finally been hired as an exorcist by the Beit Din[18], he became my boss. Years later, he was still my direct supervisor and my only real contact with the organization as a whole. Nathan only contacted me when I was in trouble, or when there was something that required my specific sort of attention.

Ze'ev, I will be in Austin tomorrow; we should meet after morning prayers and discuss your activities. Please have your expense reports as well as any notes on progress in your research since our last meeting. Remember that I have to justify your and Ms. Lana's salary as well as any purchases you have made.

It would be good if you could have Ms. Lana itemize her purchases with explanations for each line, as well as what progress has been made because of said purchases.

Rabbi Schulman

Seems I was in trouble; that was a relief. I didn't

17 Jewish religious school, focuses on Torah and Talmud

18 A counsel of three judges.

think I could handle any more dangerous situations than I was already dealing with right now. I glanced at the clock: morning prayers, I would need to leave almost immediately in order to make that, but I was already operating on minimal sleep and it would not do to make a second ten-hour drive through a pines-shrouded road without getting rest.

> *Nathan, I won't make that, I'm in Memphis and have to spend the night here. Make it a late lunch or dinner thing and I'll meet you—there's a new kosher burger food truck downtown, maybe we could try that? As for Rivkah's spending habits, as previously mentioned I am currently out of town, but I will discuss this with her at my earliest convenience.*
> *Ze'ev*

He wouldn't go for that. Nathan never ate anywhere except traditional kosher restaurants, or vegan places where he could be sure nothing was suspect—which meant that I would be unable to get a real meal for a while. I stared at the screen for a few more minutes before I closed the laptop and tossed the remainder of the pizza in the fridge to eat in the morning. If I was going to make it back to Austin tomorrow at all, I needed to get some sleep—not to mention the use of angelic names and casting had left me drained. My investigation of where the dybbuk came from would have to wait.

I was walking through a small town. It looked like Crisp, the town MeeMaw had lived in her whole life. Crisp was an hour or so south of Dallas and east of Waxahachie, practically unknown outside my dad's family. My mom had grown up in New York; her parents had fled Hungary with the help of Raoul Wallenberg during the Holocaust. My mother always joked about how her parents were both happy she found a nice 'Kaplan' farm boy and horrified that he was actually a goy and that she wanted to move to Texas to be with him. Of course, in their time Texas was where all the German POWs were taken—and with towns like Fredicksberg and New Braunfels, who can blame them? Dad's family, on the other hand, had moved to Texas and started farming goats and the land back in the 1800s. My dad never got in the way of my Mom raising me or my sisters Jewish, but he himself never converted. He always claimed that he had walked too far along his present path towards God, and that it wouldn't do to go back down the mountain just to take a different trail. It hadn't been easy growing up in that area in the lone Jewish family

Crisp boasted a population smaller than most elementary school birthday parties, and a cemetery that housed far more people—mostly family—than Crisp had ever had living in it at any given time. This wasn't actually Crisp; not the one I remembered, anyway.

This Crisp reminded me of something I had realized a long time ago. In Texas, there is a juxtaposition of progress and stagnation. I have left bustling metropolises and driven for less than an hour before coming to a broken-down farm, rotting from the inside out in the shade of some massive tree. I have seen crumbling buildings abandoned as coal or other resources dried up while driving down the highway towards an amusement park packed to the brim full of people. Here, the sheer number of people is dwarfed only by the empty spaces that surround us at all times.

Empty spaces aren't. I have seen more of the world than most, and in Texas, in the South, the empty spaces are filled with the things that no one wants to admit. Monsters of every kind: the secrets that people try to keep, the cruelty of championed idiocy and of course, the monsters that bleed through humanity's collective ignorance. If you know where to look, if you have a nose like a bloodhound's for finding them, those secrets poke up through the Texas grass-like bones emerging from a shallow grave. Hidden just beyond the shadows of that door hanging from the hinges of the broken-down barn are those things that you don't believe in—those things that you won't admit to yourself even the possibility of them existing.

The sun hung high in the sky unmoving, leeching the life from everything it touched with oppressive heat, leaving the smell of burnt asphalt and baking cow patties heavy in the air. I recognized the street names from my childhood—despite not having returned to Crisp since Bubbie's[19] mind began to slip—each one dredging memories from the hiding places into which I had shoved them years ago. Without thought, without really any means to stop

---

19 Yiddish term for Grandmother.

myself, I found myself walking down Union Hill towards Highway 660, drawn inexplicably towards one of those abandoned farm homes. The roof had caved in years ago, exposing the ribcage of a home that had lost its heartbeat and breath decades ago. I knew this particular house. I knew it very well; nearly twenty years ago as a boy, I had learned the true nature of the world around us at the home that now loomed before me.

It looked every bit as vast and foreboding as it had years ago, the paint faded and cracked, peeling away from the wood that showed the rot of countless years' neglect. I knew what I would find behind the barn, I didn't want to go back there, but my legs weren't listening to me. They carried me past the torn-down doors and into the musty shadows; debris littered the floor, and I found myself wondering again, what had happened here? For this place to be abandoned, leaving the trappings of a life where they lay, scavenged by squatters and animals? In one corner of the barn lay the skeletal corpse of a cow, still chained to a post—even in death the flies covered it, buzzing loud enough to create a constant droning in the air. When I was a child the sight of a skeletal animal would have terrified me. Now I had seen things that were far worse; so long as the corpse stayed still I could pretty much ignore it. Seeing something freshly dead would be more upsetting, because that would mean that whatever had killed could be close enough to be dangerous. Old and desiccated meant whatever had killed the cow was long gone—in theory, anyway. You can never rule everything out. I passed the corpse, as I did years ago, skirting around as far as I could—back then I was more worried about biting horseflies than bones; back then I was ignorant and braver. I knew what was coming around that corner; as soon as my feet finished walking me across the threshold, nothing would be the same.

"That is true, Ze'ev Ben Daveed[20]." My feet stopped moving, and my eyes were suddenly under my own control again. My eyes snapped up towards the voice; it had come from the far corner of the barn, and a man I didn't recognize stepped out of the shadows. He was emaciated, his skin like pallid leather stretched over bones like a grotesque chair. He wore a black suit complete with tie, and a wilted rose was pinned to his lapel. When he smiled, it was awful—more like the rictus of a corpse than anything living. His voice barely came across the room like a whisper—as though he were miles away—but somewhere in that voice was strength and steel.

"Who are you?" It was a simple but pertinent question; something was controlling my movement, and both the fact that I couldn't remember how I had arrived in Crisp and that they knew the significance of this place spoke volumes to their power—and a frightening knowledge of my life. The figure shrugged and moved more into the light. Despite everything, the man looked painfully familiar to me. He gestured with a gaunt hand towards the doorway before which I was stopped.

"You stand here, at a fork in the road, so to speak; you know what happens if you continue on the current path, what is out there." I thought I could

---

20 Ze'ev's full Hebrew name, as opposed to his legal name: Ze'ev Moses Kaplan"

almost detect a bit of a New York accent from him. He was right. My eyes moved, following the curve of shadows cast by a suddenly setting sun, out the door to the edge of an abyss. "And if you decide that life isn't for you—if you were to step back and away—who knows what your, or anyone else's, life will be?" I looked back, but the man was gone.

The doorway led to the back of the barn, hidden from the roads by a line of trees that hemmed in the plot of land where the cows would graze, when there had been living cows there. The frame was falling apart from dry rot, and even from where I stood the smell of mold and wood filled my nostrils.

Stepping across that line of shadow and light all those many years ago is why I was here now. It was why I was whisked away to Yeshiva and taught things that no child should have to learn. What I had seen then in my childhood created, in no uncertain terms, the man I am today. If I could undo that, what sort of healthy life could I lead? I wouldn't have had to say goodbye to so many people, or have seen so many hurt. I wouldn't be answering to Nathan or anyone other than some nine-to-five boss. My life could be normal, and all of this could be someone else's problem. For all intents and purposes, on one side of the door was innocence and my childhood; on the other was something else. Was it a loss of innocence? A chance encounter—or was it something far more meaningful? Could I buck a greater calling purely for a chance at personal freedom? But this choice wasn't one I was making; it was a choice I had made, a long time ago. Steeling myself, I stepped through into the light.

I jolted upright with a shout; my skin was clammy, and I was having trouble breathing as I looked around the dark hotel room. I was still in Memphis; slowly, reality came back to me, trying its best to cover the thing I had been forced to see yet again. A thing that screamed with too many mouths and bled from too many eyes. I gripped my head in my hands, willing the image out. Too many nights of nightmares had already been wasted on it; there was a time that I walked through that door every night—that sleep was very nearly a stranger. The stranger with the wilted rose on his lapel was new. Too many nights, facing down the nightmares that don't hold to the world of dreams—but any change to the dream was disturbing. I would need to meditate on it when I had more time. The room came into focus around me, horrible shapes and leering faces resolved themselves into chairs, drapes and all of the other little things that look different in the darkness of night.

It was 4:00 in the morning, and I wouldn't be getting any more sleep; history had taught me that if I tried to go back to sleep, my ability to block out the images of the past would fall away and I would be dragged back into the nightmare over and over again. Grabbing a couple of slices of pizza from the fridge, I sat on the edge of the bed, facing the large window. Outside the world still slumbered; only the very earliest of risers were beginning to stir for the day ahead of them. I caught sight of myself in my reflection.

I was in goodish shape for a man about to enter his thirties, perhaps a bit on the lean side. My right leg bore a circle of scars from a tzavua[21] across the calf that refused to grow hair; I was lucky that no one had noticed its resemblance to a bite mark so far. My chest and stomach were cross crossed with the fine scars from claws and knives; there was an old pucker in my shoulder where I had taken a round from a rifle during the Second Intifada. I was lucky that I hadn't been cut or sliced across my face, yet—though I was missing a bit of my left ear, courtesy of a mazzik[22]. All across my body I could see the scars of a dangerous life; serving in the Israeli army for a few years—followed by a career of dealing with monsters and spirits—certainly hadn't been kind to me. But I knew others who were less lucky than I was; there was a Catholic priest in San Antonio who was bound to a wheelchair now, after crossing Baalrachius—the self-proclaimed king of ghouls. I still had all of my limbs and my faith . . . which put me in a better place than a lot of the people in my profession.

I pulled on a collared shirt and jeans before reaching into my duffel bag to grab my Tefillin[23], tallit[24], and a small copy of the Armed Forces edition of the Torah[25] and Siddur[26]; even if it was only four in the morning, even if I didn't feel particularly spiritual,

21 A brightly colored hyena-like monster.

22 "Damager" A type of destructive spirit or demon.

23 Small boxes that are wrapped around the limbs for prayer

24 A Prayer shawl

25 Jewish bible

26 Prayer book

or if Nathan thought I wasn't religious enough, I would say my prayers—morning, afternoon, and night. I had come face to face with the divine and the unclean too many times to discount the existence of something much larger than myself. Often I was asked, how can I continue to be Jewish if a Catholic priest's exorcism works. How can I ignore the powers of a Taoist sorcerer, or the fact that I have seen with my own eyes things that people would worship? *Atah gabor l'olam Adonai.*[27] No matter what happens, or what I see, I know that all things come from and are HaShem.

There is a beautiful story in the Talmud[28] where a young mystic is watching a temple to some pagan god. He continues to see sick and injured people go into the temple and come out healed of their ailments. It perplexes the young man. He has learned his entire life that all other gods are false—that even praying to angels of HaShem was a sin of idolatry. He felt his faith bending, coming near snapping. After all, if these gods were false, or demonic, how were the priests able to work miracles? Why were people leaving healthy? The young man went and prayed, hoping that some vision or dream would come to him—but of course, nothing came. Finally in his desperation, faith flagging, he went to his rabbi.

"Why would HaShem allow these priests to heal people?" the young mystic asked. The rabbi smiled— likely in the infuriating way at which rabbis seem so good—and answered, in the way of rabbis, with a question.

---

27 "Yours is the only strength in the world" Common Jewish prayer.

28 Books of law and explanation for the Torah and Mishnah

"Should HaShem withhold the hour of healing, simply because they are in another's house?"

I love this story, personally; I think about it often, whenever I am faced with creatures from mythologies different than my own. Whenever I see those holy men from other faiths performing miracles, and I am forced to face the darkness that is out there. The story, to me, means that HaShem doesn't care about faith or allegiances; when the hour of healing comes, it's carried out. Sometimes, I am blessed enough to be the agent of that healing.

I say my shacharit[29], wrapped in my prayer shawl and tefillin, before finishing off the rest of the pizza. I should do a light workout; as I said, the job isn't the safest one, and being able to run just a little bit faster than whatever is chasing me has saved my ass more often than I would like to admit. But the sun is already coming up, and if I leave now, I can be back in Austin before too late and get this meeting with Nathan over with.

Carefully packing everything back up, I checked out and got ready for a grueling, boring drive through the pine forests of the South back towards home.

---

29 Morning Prayers

CHAPTER II

NATHAN TEXTED ME as I was making my drive, informing me where to meet: the grocery store in north Austin with the kosher deli; hardly surprising. The local Chabad[30], Rabbi Levertov, oversaw the deli there. Something of a hardass—but good for the Jewish community in Texas—Levertov is exactly like Nathan in so many ways. I informed him that I had left Memphis and would let him know as soon as I could meet up. The rest of the ride was just me and Tom Waits' raspy voice to keep me company. The drive between Austin, Texas and Memphis, Tennessee is a tedious trek through nothing. Pine trees were on either side of me as far across the horizon I could see. One had to be careful not to lose yourself watching the rows of trees and the stripes of the highway, especially when you only had a few hours of sleep. Luckily the large cup of truck stop coffee was keeping me as awake as I could hope to be. The bitterness made each sip a challenge, but I didn't drink the stuff because I found it enjoyable. Under normal circumstances on a long journey like this, I would welcome the opportunity to contemplate in peace, or to steel myself for an upcoming

30 Ultra-Orthadox Judaism, Chasiddic movement

confrontation. But, when that confrontation is with what was once my closest friend and is now a distant and relatively hostile boss, things were a bit different.

Sometimes I wondered if undercover cops or spies had this kind of relationship with their handlers. While I'm not any James Bond, the similarities are there—I had a job I couldn't tell anyone about; I travel extensively, fighting against things that want to cause death and destruction from the shadows. I don't get gadgets, and I don't carry a silenced pistol, or even drive an awesome car that can turn into a submarine. Instead, I have a couple of amulets, a handful of prayers and a baseball bat for when things get too hairy. Assignments almost always came from a gathering of rabbis referred to as the Beit Din—which of course was not very accurate; it would be like calling the United States Senate a triumvirate.

Traditionally the Beit Din was three rabbis acting as judges in religious matters and cases of halachah[31]. This, on the other hand, was in actuality a small organization made up of Jews from every denomination who had real brushes with the supernatural and came out the other end changed. Many of our leaders were Kabbalists[32] whose encounters were limited to touching the divine while meditating or in prayer—no easy feat in and of itself, but certainly a different breed than operatives like myself who had faced down the darkness. There were operatives like me, hunters and exorcists. In the field, we also had a few craftsmen—people who were good at a trade and could turn it to esoteric pathways.

---

31 Jewish religious law

32 Jewish mystics

Above all of us laypeople, there were people like Nathan—and, other than assigning me work and teaching, I had no idea what Nathan did. We had a small network of rabbis who acted as a governing body, but at the top of it all was an honest-to-god beit din.

I didn't know who those three were—maybe Nathan did, though I doubted it. I really should talk to Nathan about that submarine thing; this job definitely needed more perks. *(Health care was top notch, and included dental.)* The secrecy of who was at the top of the ladder of the Beit Din was no grand evil conspiracy, at least not that I knew—but we had made enough enemies of small cults, warlocks, and demons to need to be somewhat careful with our secrets. So, we tended to operate in secrecy—not because what we were doing was wrong, but because knowledge of the supernatural would be dangerous. Not only for the people we were trying to protect; not everything out there that was inhuman was dangerous, and they were all HaShem's creations. The last thing this world needed was for some dimwit in a blond toupee to decide that it was time to reenact the witch hunts.

Memphis-to-Austin is about a ten-hour drive, if you don't make any stops—and while I did need to meet with Nathan, I wasn't in a rush to make it super convenient for him, especially not at the cost of my own mental health. Once you hit a certain point, the endless forests of pine give way to endless flat plains and pastures: North Texas farmland, even more dangerous for sleep-deprived individuals suffering from nightmares. I pulled into a small Thai restaurant off the highway in Dallas, stuffed my face with drunken noodles and chugged down two Thai iced coffees. These were sweetened with condensed milk, refreshing and caffeinated to keep me going—maybe a bit too caffeinated, actually.

I felt antsy as I left, and my mind turned back towards Sarah Cohen and the dybbuk. It was at once more and less dramatic than my own introduction to the supernatural, which had tainted my own being with whatever taint calls out to mythic and mystic beings. Small Texas towns, even outside of big ones like Dallas, are home to bad secrets and terrible shames—not even considering the things in the shadows. I didn't have a lot of friends as a kid—a lot of moms kept their kids away from us; they didn't trust our weird prayers, or the fact we always drove into Dallas on Saturdays to go to "Jew Church." But Mikey Donovan was always a good friend; he was the kid with whom I would explore the fields, or go craw-dadding when the ditches were full of water from the rain. But Mikey's dad was a mean drunk, and one evening he was too mean, and too drunk. Of course, I didn't find out right away; I found out after Mikey had been missing from class for a week. But that didn't mean much to me at first; Mikey had been coming over to play every day between when his dad killed him and the news breaking. After I found out what had happened, Mikey became less playful each time he appeared. More and more insistent that he needed *help*.

After a few weeks of being haunted, Mikey possessed me. His dybbuk hitched a ride in me, in an attempt to make a grab at all of the life he was denied.

My parents had no idea how to deal with this; the church community my dad belonged to couldn't wrap their heads around something wrong that couldn't be solved by screaming out Jesus' name at me over and over again. It wasn't until my mom called Bubbie and Zeyde[33] in Brooklyn that they found the answers they were looking for. Rabbi Marty flew all the way down to Texas and talked Mikey out of it. I didn't know it at the time, but that was my first brush with the Beit Din. After that it was even harder for me and my sister to make friends. Everyone thought we had been possessed by Satan himself. They were lonely times for me, and that led to more and more introversion and exploring the old farms and barns by myself. But after that possession, I became a magnet for the supernatural. I would see dybbuks and sheydim just outside the streetlights and hiding in the shadows. And eventually that magnetism—and the death of my father—would lead me to the encounter in the barn.

I shook myself back to the present; caffeine usually doesn't debilitate me too much, but as I finished the last leg of the drive from Dallas to Austin, I was nearly nauseous with feelings of foreboding and paranoia. I could feel my stomach tying itself into knots with the promise of calamity. Maybe I was more nervous about this meeting that I thought. Every gut instinct I had was lit up by the caffeine. Anxiety is a bizarre physiological response—making us feel like someone is watching us, about to strike, when in reality everything is fine.

The feelings stuck with me throughout the rest of the drive, and as I drove into Austin I realized that I

---

33 Yiddish term for Grandfather

was a little bit of a mess—nothing that a hot shower and a shave to clean up the beard couldn't fix. I didn't want to give Nathan any more fuel for disapproval, so even though it was out of my way I headed to my apartment before going to meet him. I texted Nathan to let him know I would be about an hour late and continued down south.

I live far south—near enough to the major highways to get wherever I needed to go, and far enough out from the city center that I could afford to live on my salary. The biggest downside to living in South Austin is isolation. Nearly the entire Jewish community of central Texas was concentrated up north, near the Dell Jewish Community Center. Three congregations, a school, the community center itself, a kosher deli inside the local grocery chain and the presence of the local Chabad meant that when community was happening, it happened up north. Even my synagogue was a bit of a drive. But the neighbors were always lovely, and I could take care of all my basic needs without venturing too far from home. There were tacos, a lady who sold tamales door to door and enough live music within walking distance to make up for the somewhat low-income area in which I made my nest. To top it all off, it was close to the small office space I rented for my and Rivkah's research.

Rivkah Lana is my assistant—or more appropriately, she's an operative like me. But she isn't cut out for fieldwork, so instead she stays back and researches lore and scientific answers to mystical problems. Before her first brush with a pack of blood-hungry sheydim, Rivkah had been a phenomenal doctoral student studying engineering and biochemistry. From what I had been able to follow, she had been studying the way elements interacted differently according to compounding them in different ways—over my head, honestly. I had considered studying metallurgy at one point; the idea of crafting swords had struck a chord with the wild teenager in me. I suppose that was my ren-fair phase: I knew about the existence and prevalence of supernatural and unnatural creatures, but I hadn't been through the fires of mystical rebirth at that point. I had never gone through with it. My father would never have allowed a forge on the farm when he was alive. Now Rivkah worked for me—not the best trade-off for her, I'll be the first to admit. But it did work out great for me; she was decent with metallurgy and basic first aid, which cut down on my own prep time and hospital bills. Having a home base with someone who could do research, and help create talismans, and gather the odder things needed for various spell work was nothing to spurn—and I suppose at the end of the day the Beit Din was funding her new research; despite Nathan's protests, her requests for equipment and studies had never been turned down.

I pulled into the Landry Place apartments, which sprawled a bit—two stories at its tallest, with a small pool and workout room at the center. I was never able to find a parking space close to my apartment, a symptom of the place being filled by UT kids living on their parents' dimes; after parking I had to walk for a few minutes to get to my apartment. The first thing I noticed stepping inside was that the light was on. Forgetting to turn off the lights isn't something that I do, but that wasn't all; I am by no means a neat freak, and I tend to keep notes, books, and whatever I happen to be working on strewn about the apartment wherever I happened to last work on it. Even still, my apartment was a mess. Drawers had been pulled out and emptied, and furniture was overturned; I had been robbed.

I gritted my teeth; it seemed like just my luck: I leave town for a single night to take care of work and my home gets burgled. I scanned the front room to see if anything was gone; I expected the TV or maybe my computer to be missing, but everything seemed present and accounted for. I moved carefully through the debris, eyes scanning for anything that could give some hint as to why I would have been targeted—other than the obvious of not being home and being Jewish. People continue to suffer under the idea that every Jew is wealthy, and the act of merely being Jewish means that you have gold bars stashed in your home. People who knew me for years still occasionally made comments about how everyone at my synagogue was a lawyer or doctor, or how when I was broke, I should be able to borrow money from my synagogue. They forget that both my parents had grown up dirt poor, and only through their hard work had I been allowed to have a better life than theirs. Maybe the thief had seen the full case of instant ramen and realized they were mistaken.

I moved down the narrow hallway to the apartment's one bedroom; I felt trepidation, like someone was watching me. For a few seconds I assumed that those feelings were coming from my lack of sleep, too much caffeine, and the knowledge that someone had broken into my safe place. The only warning that there was still danger was the sudden and fast-moving shadow out of the corner of my eye; on instinct I threw myself forward, rolling into my room and coming up in a crouch to face whatever had been behind me.

The man who had just attacked me held a wicked, curved ceremonial knife with a strip of red cloth tied around the hilt; not the sort of thing you generally found in an everyday burgling—of course, most thieves didn't try to murder their victims immediately, at least not in my experience. The man wore blue jeans that looked like they were caked in dirt, and a ratty t-shirt with some band logo on it. His skin was a dark brown, and if I had to guess, I would place him as having Indian ancestry. The most notable thing, however, was his eyes; they were wide and bloodshot, his pupils dilated to the point that I had to wonder how he could see at all. His lips were pulled back in a snarl that revealed teeth gritted tight enough to begin to crack. Drugs explained a lot; though hard drugs like PCP weren't common in Austin, they also weren't unheard of. My mind raced with possibilities—why was there a junkie with a knife in my apartment?

I didn't have much in the way of weapons in my apartment; my Jericho pistol would be in the gun case in the hallway closet, and while I knew how to use a knife in a fight, I hadn't brought any with me on my trip to Memphis. That was okay; I have always preferred a more hands-on approach when dealing with problems. I charged forward, grabbing at his knife-wielding arm with my right hand and planting my shoulder firmly in the center of his chest, pushing back with all of my might, knocking him back and down. Holding onto his wrist with my hand I pressed my momentum forward; I wanted to break his wrist or arm as quickly as possible, but had to maneuver in a way that wouldn't end with me getting gutted by the knife.

The junkie rolled with me, twisting to keep his arm from snapping, his wild eyes inches from mine for a moment before I felt his foot come up and kick me square in the chest, knocking the air out of me and forcing me back several steps and onto my ass against the kitchen counter. My feet scrabbled over the debris he had knocked onto the floor as I tried to find purchase and steady myself.

"You will not interfere with the Lord of Flesh!" His voice was sluggish and slurred; the words made no sense at all. Then again, when you work in my field, you tend to attract the attention of creatures who gave themselves ridiculous titles. So, the junkie in front of me wasn't just some random thief, but a zealot who felt like I was a threat to his master's plans. That wasn't very comforting. I used the counter to push myself up without taking my eyes off the knife-wielding man. I feinted left and watched him twitch to follow. His reflexes were amped up, and if it was because of something like PCP, I wouldn't be able to just beat him into submission. I darted forward and began to piston my fists into his sides. I could feel a rib crack under the force of my blows before I danced back and out of the range of his blade.

"Who the fuck is the 'Lord of Flesh?'" I shouted at him, hoping to make him work in two directions at once. In my line of work, sometimes things are black and white—and without fail I've been able to classify knife-wielding zealots who break into my home as being firmly in the 'bad guy' camp. I figured if I could keep this psychopath talking for long enough, I could figure out a way to overpower him. Hell, if I could get to the other side of the kitchen, I could grab a knife and at least even out the fight a little bit.

"He is the master of life and death, tyrant of the bridge between this world and the next. He summons the spirits of friend and foe, commanding an army of ended life." The zealot kept speaking, giving this 'lord of flesh' title after title. It sounded like a necromancer to me. This attack had to be related to the exorcism I had just performed in Memphis. But to be able to find my home—and send someone there to ransack it and attack me before I was even able to get there—spoke of having resources that rivaled most government agencies, or of having enough magic clout to do some scrying. Neither option was ideal, but when dealing with a cult, I would rather have to deal with some cantrip-wielding schmuck than a vast conspiracy. I realized the zealot was still talking: " . . . and he demands your blood!" I dove forward and attempted to tackle him.

The zealot's knee rocketed up and caught me just under the chin; for a moment I saw stars and fell back again, catching myself on the dining room table. I reached out to catch myself and found an empty glass bottle—maybe being messy wasn't the worst thing—and winged it at my assailant's head. I had played baseball for a bit back in my youth in between sessions of studying Torah and Talmud, and I still had a pretty decent throwing arm. The bottle whistled through the air and hit the man just above the right eye, causing him to stagger back. I followed after the bottle, taking advantage of the man's dazed expression and the blood now dripping into his eye.

This time I ignored the knife; he was dazed, and I needed to press my advantage. It took two leaping steps to reach him, and I slammed punch after punch into his face. I felt the cartilage of his nose snap under my knuckles, but I wasn't thinking clearly anymore. I saw red; this was my home, my sanctuary, and safe place. This kadokhes[34] came to me in an attempt to hurt me, and violated my inner sanctum. In my mind, I knew I should stop fighting this man—that I had defended myself—but my rage wouldn't let me stop, and my fist kept flying. He fell back under my constant barrage; my breath was coming in deep gulps as I tried to get hold of my anger—I didn't want to kill him, I just wanted to pacify him until the cops could show up.

Surprising me completely, the zealot suddenly lurched forward, his face a near-unrecognizable mass of welts and bruises; he spared one look at me before dashing for the door. I didn't want to let him escape, and started forward before falling to a knee. I suddenly realized I hadn't been as lucky as I had thought; at some point during my assault, the zealot had scored several cuts on my arms and chest. The adrenaline wearing off brought on painful awareness of the pain that protested my every move, and the fact

---

34 Yiddish insult meaning worthless person

that my clothes were now soaked in blood. Great, more scars; my knuckles were beginning to swell, too—and to top it all off, I had to clean this whole mess. I moved to the door and glared around the parking lot, but the man was nowhere to be seen. I went inside and called the cops; it would be up to them to catch the lunatic now. And maybe a quick trip to the hospital wasn't a terrible idea.

CHAPTER III

AFTER THE RUN-IN at my house, Nathan was more understanding as to why I was so late to our meeting. I walked into the HEB up north and ordered a burger from the kosher deli inside. I could feel Nathan's eyes boring into my back as I put in my order, and then I finally came and sat down at the table with him. He watched me, disdain for the man I had become warring with concern on his face. He may be a cantankerous man who took himself too seriously and had a stick up his ass, but he was also a spiritual leader, and in the end, he couldn't help himself.

"You look terrible, Ze'ev; are you all right?"

I nodded haphazardly—I wasn't, of course, but I had to pretend so we could get through this meeting as quickly as possible. The hours of driving, lack of sleep, getting in that fight and then the trip to the hospital afterwards was not treating me particularly well. I had stitches where I had been cut, and my hands were wrapped and bandaged. The only good news was that stitches meant that any new scarring would be minimal.

I set the paperwork Nathan had requested in front of me and slid it across the table. He took it and thumbed through it, not taking his eyes off my face. "You said you were attacked in your home?"

I nodded. "Yeah, and I think it's work-related."

He shot me an annoyed look. "Why should it be work-related?"

"Why shouldn't it be?" I shot back. "The man that attacked me said he was working for a necromancer. That sounds related to what I do, doesn't it? I mean, he wasn't just a psychopath breaking into homes; the thing in Memphis wasn't a confused and lost Dybbuk—it was brought, it was summoned, and it was malicious."

Nathan nodded, chewing his lip before reaching up to run his fingers through his beard thoughtfully.

"We wouldn't normally go against human practitioners, but if he is using magic to harass and endanger Jewish families, they are not leaving us much choice—and attacking you in your home . . . " Nathan sighed and spread his hands in a gesture that said he wish he had more answers.

"That was my thinking," I agreed, "but if this dybbuk and this attack are related it means that not only is there a necromancer—there is a decently powerful magician who isn't hesitating to hurt and even kill people that he perceives as being in his way . . . I think I should pay a visit to Shanocht; it would have noticed if someone was grave-robbing or messing with the dead."

Nathan's face hardened, but I had known that was coming and was ready for his judgment. "You shouldn't deal with that thing, it isn't proper, and it certainly isn't sanctioned!"

I nodded, I knew everything he was saying was right, but sometimes the usual paths to information weren't good enough. I waved away his annoyance.

"Ze'ev, you're going to get yourself killed."

"And then where would you be, Nathan, needing to find a new exorcist in the great state of Texas; would you have to come and handle things yourself?" He paled a little at my question. "You and I both know that the only reason you deal with me at all is because you don't have enough resources to replace me."

"That isn't true, Ze'ev; you're good at what you do, you're a good . . . " Was he about to say friend, and then stopped himself? " . . . man," he finished lamely. I let my frustration hang in the air for a moment before moving on. Perhaps I was being unfair to Nathan; not everything he said was a jab at work or my Jewishness, but it often felt like that. I gestured to the paperwork in front of him.

"Let's just go through this, so I can get back to being good at what I do."

"Lunch" with Nathan lasted a couple of hours, going through the ins and outs of various reports and activities. Once we got down to business, Nathan wasn't nearly as insufferable. Focusing on the job, protecting people, mystical research, trying to interpret dreams or visions from meditation sessions—these were things that reignited the feelings of friendship, things that we could get lost in. After it was over, I finally decided to give Sara a call. As I assumed, as soon as I told Sara what had happened—leaving out a few details, of course—she demanded that I come over so she could baby me. Raised a good Jewish girl, she had left religion without entirely abandoning the traditions that made Judaism a culture as much as it was a faith. She was a dream; a petite woman whose drive to stay healthy meant that she stayed in ridiculously good shape, and could keep up with me when I hit the hiking trail or gym—something I did almost as often as she did, so that I could make sure I could run when the cards were down. She had large brown eyes and full lips that complimented her frequent smiles, all framed by long blond hair. Best of all, she had a fantastic sense of humor and would laugh easily. I needed that sense of frivolity and levity in my life.

Being a health nut, Sara frequently cooked delicious, healthy food to share with me. My cooking was nothing special; I had learned to cook while serving in the army, and so my meals tended to be practical and straightforward—not that I preferred that; my Bubbie and my mother had both been amazing cooks. Sara's food was a far cry from the fatty brisket and chicken-fried-steak I loved as a child, but it was healthier and tasted great nonetheless. Sara's food, like her laughter, kept me feeling alive and reenergized me.

The final piece of the puzzle was her kindness; Sara was a loving person, working as a nurse. She spent her days caring for hospice patients. Nearly always on-call from picking up extra shifts, she was always willing and able to take care of any sob story that came her way. As I walked through her front door, one of those sob stories charged at me from another room, throwing its full fifty pounds of slobber, wrinkles, and funk at my legs.

"Hey, Tooth," I greeted the ancient bulldog,

reaching down to scratch him between the ears. Tooth had been a breeder in a puppy mill, and despite daily walks, a special diet and everything else Sara could think of, he had been unable to lose any weight. As Tooth waddled next to me as I walked further into Sara's home, I could hear his every labored breath. Sara's apartment was nicer than mine; everything in its place, everything dusted and wiped down. With how much Sara worked I had no idea how she managed to keep such a tidy home, or how she kept Tooth healthy and happy, but both always seemed to be in excellent condition. (Well, the house was in excellent condition; Tooth was just Tooth, but he was happy.)

Judging from the smell and the sound of sizzling coming from the kitchen, I could guess where Sara was. It sounded like she was likely making fajitas, a personal favorite. "Hey, honey," I called to make sure I wasn't going to startle her as I came into the room. She turned; she was crying, not what I was expecting. "Sara?" She took two long steps towards me and hit my chest with a limp-wristed closed fist. Not trying to hurt me, but definitely mad; unfortunately, she did hit a stitch. Her eyes widened when she saw me wince.

"Ze'ev Moses Kaplan." She was shout-whispering at me; she sniffed and rubbed a hand over her eyes, further mussing her mascara. "You got attacked in your home with a knife, and then you go to a meeting, and THEN you decide that maybe you should call your girlfriend to let her know?"

Ah, that was why she was so angry. Tooth grumbled and sat on my foot, recognizing the serious voices, and looked back and forth between us in great, slow-witted concern.

"Sara, I was fine; the police are handling everything, the hospital checked me out, the stitches are minimal—it's fine."

"Stitches?" She pulled up my t-shirt to look at my cuts and let out a disgusted shout before turning around and stomping back into the kitchen. "Stitches, Zev. Stitches, and while you were at the hospital you didn't think, "Oh, maybe I should call Sara, my girlfriend, and let her know I'm in the hospital?'"

I wouldn't say that I would rather deal with a coked-out fanatic than an angry girlfriend, but it felt like a pretty close call. I was at least reasonably sure Sara wasn't going to stab me, or throw a searing-hot cast iron skillet at my head.

"Sara, I knew I was going to call you as soon as my meeting was over; since I wasn't in any danger, why worry you for no reason?" I pushed a chair out and sat down slowly, exhaustion threatening to overcome me. As I did, Tooth pulled himself into my lap and snorted contentedly; he must have decided that he could ignore the emotional storm raging around him, so long as he had a lap.

We argued for what felt like hours, but was really just through dinner. I was too fatigued to keep it up, and offered my apologies for not calling her first before retreating to the shower to finally get cleaned up and wash away the grime of my last two days. The hot water steamed the glass of the shower door, and stung against my cuts and bruises. Each muscle seemed to tighten and then ease as it finally relaxed.

Most of my life really did consist of doing research

and safe practices. I traveled throughout the South and did simple protections on Jewish homes, acting as sort of a spiritual mashgiach[35]. Checking mezuzahs[36] and other ritual items to make sure they were up to snuff, I would give a few talks now and then and offer coaching. Sara thought I worked as an event coordinator with the Jewish Community Center; it allowed me to work whatever hours I needed to, and I could always explain scrapes and bruises as being a result of moving equipment. She usually pestered me about trying to find something bigger and better. But what else was I qualified for? Private security? Torah Study? Even if I did leave behind the Beit Din, I would still have to contend with my innate magnetism to the supernatural forces in the world. Also, would they attempt to put Rivkah in the field? She was a highly capable researcher and assistant, but she would be torn apart the first time she encountered a violent monster. The status quo was the best way . . . for now.

When I stepped out of the shower, Sara greeted me in a robe, a warm, mischievous smile on her face. I didn't know if that meant she forgave me or not, but Sara was the sort always to chase fighting and arguing with some physical activity. She looked gorgeous; she always did, her dark tanned skin glowing in the low light, the curve of her breasts just visible from the neck of her robe. She took the towel from me, drying my skin gently, chasing the towel with kisses here and there. No matter where my head was at or how exhausted I was, Sara was always able to awaken the

---

35 Jewish authority that oversees matters of Halachah and Kashrut

36 Blessing that is posted next to doorways in Jewish homes

animal instinct in me; it was a gift she had. Even still, I needed to be careful; it wouldn't do to hurt myself this way. But as I had told her, they were minor injuries.

I closed my eyes as she moved to her knees to continue drying and kissing, enjoying her attention as long as I could bear it before I needed her. I reached down, gently pulling her to her feet, and then tugged on her robe, taking a moment to appreciate her lithe body before I lifted her off the floor and carried her to the bed. I pushed my exhaustion away to press against her, exploring every inch of her body as we revitalized ourselves, body and soul.

My phone rang, waking me up late. I was alone; well, almost alone. Sara had left at some point on a call to the hospital. Laying on my arm and pinning me down, Tooth snored loudly. I looked at the overweight bulldog for a moment, a fellow broken soul, rescued by Sara. He had been given a second chance at life and liberty—a chance that he embraced fully, while I was still walking a path that would end with me alone. Sarah claimed that she couldn't sleep without the sound of his snores; I didn't sleep over often enough for that to be the case for me, but I did have to admit that the feeling of his rumbles and grumbles was a bit soothing. I could do without the drool and flatulence, though. I considered closing my eyes and just going back to sleep—I felt like I had earned some sleep—but the reality of the situation was that there was too much going on that I didn't know about. Besides, my phone was still ringing. Who was calling me now? Tooth let out a low, aggressive toot, helping me make my decision.

Slowly, I pulled my arm out from under the dog, who complained by snorting and rolling onto his back. I watched him settle back in for a moment before reaching for my phone, wincing as I remembered the stitches. I didn't recognize the number and considered letting it go to voicemail, but decided to answer anyway.

"Mr. Kaplan, I'm Sargent Joseph Zalot of the Austin police department. I believe we have found your attacker; would you be able to come down and identify him?"

My head wasn't completely clear, but this seemed to be pretty good news. "Uh, yeah, sure; I'll get dressed and head over to the station." I sat up slowly, careful to fight the urge to stretch. I didn't want to pop any stitches on Sara's bed. "I guess it's the station down on the Seventh Street?" I looked around for my clothes, and spotted them folded and ready to go in a chair near the bedroom door; Sara had to be an angel.

"Close; he'll be at the morgue on Sabine, not too far from the station—and no rush, Mr. Kaplan; he isn't going anywhere." I was going to ask for clarification, but the sergeant had already hung up the phone. I felt lead in my stomach; had I unintentionally killed the man in my rage? If he had run off and then succumbed to internal bleeding because of what I did, that would be guilt I would have to live with . . . along with the other guilty feelings that I kept bottled inside. Why should I feel guilty? The man attacked me with a knife in my own home! He was a drug addict bent on killing me in the service of some whacked-out necromancer! But on the other hand, I was a trained soldier; I knew how to fight and how to subdue. And I should have subdued the man myself, held onto him until the police got there; then he would still be alive. As awful as it is, I found myself hoping that he had died from an OD, or really from anything other than me. But there's no escaping responsibility—especially not in my line of work—so I pulled on my clothes, gave Tooth a few belly scratches, and headed out of the door.

CHAPTER IV

A S I DROVE, I considered the possibility of the man passing away due to his injuries from our fight. If it was determined that he died due to the injuries he sustained from me, I could be facing some charges; more than that, I would have to answer to the Beit Din about what had happened. It was self-defense, so I shouldn't be exiled or shunned. The question, of course, would be whether or not I used excessive force. Above all, Judaic law stipulates that a person has the right to defend themselves and protect their life. But, both also want to ensure that you don't go beyond protecting yourself. When does self-defense slip into murder? When did necessity slip into rage? I wished that the Sergeant had stayed on the phone a little bit longer so that I could find out more information. He probably wouldn't have; it was probably protocol to not disclose more information than "show up at the morgue and identify the body." It is what it is, and it was what it was. The man was dead, and whatever the cause, I would have to face the consequences of that.

It turned out that the medical examiner's office was close to the police station. I parked under the bridge at I35 and Seventh Street before walking the few blocks to the morgue. The building itself was a three-story block; a stone exterior did nothing to make me feel more welcome. A stout-looking fence and gate blocked off the back of the building, and the sidewalk was hemmed in by a short wall, all giving the impression of being funneled into the building. I'm not claustrophobic, but the atmosphere was stifling even before entering. I guess it's pretty par-for-the-course, but I feel like a place where people have to go to find out if their loved ones have been killed or died should be more comforting—maybe provide some therapeutic scenery, smells, or music.

Stepping inside, I looked around the clinical-looking waiting room and at the nervous-looking kid who was sitting behind the desk right in front of me. I had been in morgues before, and this one seemed pretty standard—a far cry from the flickering lights and death traps that you would see in movies and TV shows. It occurred to me, somewhere in my lizard brain, that this was a dangerous place no matter how it looked—but one could not avoid the police and their suspicion at the same time, and so I approached the desk and stood in front of the young man. I half wondered if he was an intern; he seemed too young to be working in the real world yet. But then again, since hitting 30 everyone under 30 looks too young to be anything other than in grade school.

"Can I help you?" His eyes hadn't left me since I entered, and from the way he nearly trembled, I had to assume he was fighting through some heavy social anxiety. I can be nice when I want to be, but I also usually don't see the point. I had things to do, and the sooner I finished this the sooner I could set up a meeting with Shanocht—this was a day of unpleasant errands and horrible places. At least I got to go to sleep under pleasant circumstances; my mind threatened to wander back into that happy and warm place with Sara. I shook my head to dislodge thoughts that would cloud my judgment and my actions.

I shook my head to dislodge thoughts that would cloud my judgment and my actions. "Ze'ev Kaplan; I'm here to identify a body, Sergeant Zalot called." The man nodded and stood, fumbling with keys as he rose to take me back. I ignored him, too tired to be amused by his antics, and leaned over to fill out the visitor log.

"Oh! No need to do that, since, um, Sergeant Zalot called you in." He reached over and pulled the sign-in sheet away from me before walking around the office to lead me to another room, presumably where the body of my attacker was being kept. "Mondays are slow; we're busier on weekends so, just me right now." He gave off a chuckle before unlocking a door. "He'll be right in here." I nodded, stepping through the door and turning to face him.

"Has the coroner announced cause of death yet?" I held my breath, waiting for the inevitable proclamation of my guilt to fall from his lips.

"Ah, no, not officially; we were hoping you would identify him before we went forward with the examination." I let out the breath that I was holding. The explanation seemed reasonable enough, so I stepped back and waited for him to join me. To my surprise, he shook his head. "I uh, need to stay near the door in case anyone comes in, but, you can, I mean, I trust you, so, just do, I mean identify him, and I'll lock up after you finish." And with that, he retreated letting the door swing closed behind him. I had to wonder if the kid had any social graces at all. He must be an intern. I had never been left alone with a room full of dead bodies before; well, not intentionally—not by people connected to the police department. Even when I was in the military, there was always someone over my shoulder making sure that I didn't contaminate something or mess with something I shouldn't. I never took it personally; it's just the way things are. Maybe it should have been my first warning, telling me to trust my lizard brain gut, that this place was full of danger.

The room itself looked more like I would expect from a typical morgue: examination tables, several drawers for bodies, a deep bone-chilling cold, and of course, the overpowering smell of chemicals. At least the room was well-lit, though the lab equipment and surgical tools that were visible from where I stood gave it a sinister vibe. There was one body out of the drawers, laying on a slab with a sheet covering it from head to toe. That had to be the body of my attacker. At least I hoped it was; if it wasn't I would not only have gotten someone else's dearly departed—not that he was dearly departed for me—but I would also have to do a hide-and-go-seek scavenger hunt for the body of my attacker. I approached the body with only a little trepidation; I had served in the Israeli army, I had been at the heart of human catastrophe and seen death and destruction eye-to-eye. This would only be difficult if I were the cause of his death. Even then, I was no medical examiner, I was no medic or doctor; I wouldn't actually be able to tell what killed the man unless it was glaringly obvious.

As I reached for the sheet covering the body, my senses began to scream at me; everything here was wrong—the nervous man who didn't have me sign in, being left alone in this room . . . I jerked my hand back from the still form of the man and held my breath. No explosions, no knife-wielding maniacs emerged. I was being paranoid—a by-product of being attacked in my own home for sure, but not always the correct reaction. I quelled my anxiety and reached forward to pull the sheet free. The corpse reacted with startling quickness, grabbing my arm and letting out a hate-filled moan as it began to sit up.

Sometimes paranoia was utterly justified.

Panicking, I fell back, wrenching my arm free. In the seconds that followed, my mind raced to try to figure out what was happening. My first thought was that the zealot had laid a trap for me to finish the job; it was definitely the same man from yesterday. His face was still swollen from the punches I had landed, and he was wearing the same clothes. I dismissed that option reasonably quickly, as the man in front of me was also definitely dead. His eyes were dull and lifeless, not focusing on me, even as his head turned to follow my movements. His hand had been cold and clammy when he had grabbed me, and he was moving with the sort of halting movements that I had only seen before when sorcery was combating rigor mortis. It occurred to me in that moment that it's unacceptable that I know what sorcery combating rigor mortis looks like; no one else had to deal with having this knowledge.

I had beaten this man before, but he had been alive and able to feel pain and fear before. Magic—as a broad subject—was wild, and you never could guess what someone outside your tradition could do. Without knowing what sort of spell or at least what mystical tradition the necromancer was following, I couldn't know what I was up against. This corpse could be incredibly durable, breath fire, drain energy, or any number of other nasty surprises. My best option was to book it out the door and get away from it as quickly as possible. I ran to the door and pulled on it, fully expecting to fling the door open; it didn't budge. I could see the shadow of a man on the other side, and the voice of the nervous receptionist called out to answer my frantic door rattling: "Master Basken sends his greetings!"

That figured; the little shit was some punk-ass that followed the cult, that's why nothing was being done the right way. I grit my teeth as I answered. "Let me out of here. You know this can't end well for you!"

His shadow on the other side of the door was already retreating. I started to shout more after him when a sudden impact threw me forward and into the door; I was stunned but otherwise unhurt. In my pocket, something burned like a cigarette lighter scorching my leg. The amulet I had carried to protect myself from physical harm had dampened most of the impact. I had decided to carry it after the attack in my home. Sometimes my foresight is in complete shit; I didn't know if my amulet had saved my life just then, but it probably had if you factor in the condition I would've been after that attack.

I scrambled up around a table, looking to put

anything between myself and the corpse that was focused on breaking me. With an examination slab between us, I thrust my hand into my pocket; just as I feared, my amulet had cracked in half—a side effect of absorbing too much energy all at once, rendering it useless. That meant that other than my wits, I was virtually unprotected now. It also meant that if the creature had landed that hit, it probably would have broken my spine. So, the thing was supernaturally strong; that meant that its strength was probably purely magical.

The thing that had once been a man hissed at me and bound onto the table between us. It was behaving like a feral beast, it had enhanced strength, and it wanted to kill me. Somewhere in the back of my mind, I sorted this information away for later analysis—ever the optimist that there would be a later. I lashed out with a fist, connecting with a satisfying crack that whipped the zombie's head to the side. Without missing a beat, it swiped back at me; I was able to turn and take the hit on the shoulder, still taking enough force to send me tumbling across the room. I took a second to recalibrate my position and try to spot anything I could use to my advantage. I could feel blood soaking my shirt where my stitches had torn. I needed to end this as quickly as possible. It would be just my luck that I would bleed out during a fight with the zombie.

My eyes fell on a bone saw. I leaped over a table, working to keep ahead of the undead by any means necessary. Wrapping my fingers around the handle of the blade, I turned to face the zombie once again. It was on me in a second, fingers curled into claws that swiped and tore at the air, reaching for me. I swung the saw to meet its hand, grinning as the blade tore through its dead flesh as easily as its knife had cut into mine yesterday. Two of its fingers landed on the ground, but my victory was short-lived as its other hand came up and grabbed my head and slammed it into one of the aluminum tables nearby. Again, I was lucky; if the table had been anything with less give, I would have been killed or at least knocked out instead of dazed. The zombie's face came close to mine as it held me there, and somewhere deep within its empty eyes, I could almost feel something watching me from far away. It brought up its now-injured hand to finish me off, and without any other option, I opened my lips and whispered the true pronunciation of the silent aleph[37].

Rabbis argue over what was created first—if it was souls, angels; if the darkness itself was created before anything. But before HaShem created anything more literal, like light or worlds—before the first template of humanity was formed from dust—the words of Creation were brought into existence. Perhaps Hebrew is not the actual language of Creation, but it is the language I personally use to tap into that spark of the divine within me. Magic—and all power—comes from HaShem; methods of tapping into it vary in how successful they are, and how safe they are. The true pronunciation of letters (or in theory, words) had the truest connection to that power, and offered the direst consequences.

The world stopped as the last non-sound left my lips; a shockwave pushed out, throwing the zombie

---

37 The first letter of the Hebrew alphabet, silent.

like a ragdoll across the room; glass shattered and tables overturned away from me, objects warping and becoming displaced in space and time. The entire morgue buckled against me as I forced my will as a creator on it, and as quickly as it happened, the rules of physics as set forth during the Creation of reality snapped back in place. I rolled off the table, catching myself on my hands and knees, and spat blood. My throat was a raw mess of torn flesh, blood and phlegm. The sound was not an easy thing to utter, and my body was paying the price, but it had given me a few moments of which to take advantage.

I stood shakily and grabbed a scalpel from a nearby tray before moving to the prone zombie and straddling it. In its forehead, I carved three Hebrew letters: aleph, mem and tav. The corpse was beginning to regain its power; as my willpower retreated back into me, the magic of the necromancer came flooding back.

"Za emet[38]!" I growled, striking down at the word I had carved, tearing the scalp away; in effect erasing the aleph, changing 'emet', meaning truth, into 'met,' the Hebrew word for death. As soon as the word was changed, the creature stopped struggling. My own magic, physically on the body of the corpse, had overpowered whatever connection the necromancer had maintained. Slowly the now-defunct corpse's head fell to the side, mouth lolling open. Something that looked like small, reddish grains of rice fell out of its mouth; whatever they were, they could be a clue towards the magic and the identity of the group trying to kill me. I scooped the grains off the ground and slipped them into a pocket.

---

38 "This is truth"

I moved to the door and pressed my luck; my willpower still existed in the vicinity, and I focused my mind on the door. It had been locked—but if it had been locked at many points, it had also been unlocked at many points. Through the willpower I exerted on the world, the door was now unlocked. I stepped outside; the cultist playing receptionist had fled, probably as soon as he locked the door. Just as well that he didn't have me sign in; I had to imagine that the Sergeant Zalot I had spoken to on the phone either was not actually a cop, or wasn't actually acting on official duty. If Zalot existed and was a member of the cult, that would mean the police wouldn't know I had been here. With a now beaten and mutilated corpse in the morgue, there would be extremely difficult questions to answer. Not having my name signed into the visitor log would give me a little more time before the cops were on me.

I am pretty sure that when most people think about exorcists, they think of sweeping Catholic cathedrals. When they think of Jews, they probably think about Chasidim like Nathan, or maybe synagogues or even libraries. They probably didn't think of small offices in the back of a business park off the highway. I parked outside the door and was happy to see Rivkah's little Prius sitting in its own parking space. I needed her help now. Using three different keys, I unlocked the front door and walked in, taking the time to re-lock the door before glancing around the office space. It was really more of a small warehouse than it was an office. Several bookshelves were holding esoteric and rare tomes; a worktable was covered in metal and ceramic working tools, and there was plenty of storage. Off to one side, I had a large dry erase board on which I worked out various magical formulae and formations. In the back was Rivkah's workstation, which looked like it combined the very best of medieval kabbalistic alchemy and modern science. She did a lot of work on alchemy, given her background in chemistry. She was busy and didn't notice me at first—she was bent over a book, probably on some sort of study of how the elements were explained in relationship to angels.

Rivkah was small—well, small in stature. She stood around 5' 2" but had an hourglass figure that could easily cause whiplash in people driving past. Rivkah was definitely not what people thought of when they thought of a nice Jewish girl. Besides her dangerously distracting curves, she was covered in tattoos. I had never seen her in less than her standard tank-top / jeans-with-a-cardigan combo; even so, every inch of skin below her neck that was visible was tatted up in beautiful and colorful designs. I sometimes teased her about secretly being yakuza. The sides of her head were shaved, with what hair she kept resembling a loose and wavy mohawk—it wouldn't look out of place in a sci-fi movie even before she dyed it purple. Then there were the piercings: right eyebrow, ears (so many times), left nostril and tongue. Today she was wearing shimmering smoke-colored eyeshadow and black lipstick. No, she wasn't your average brilliant chemist or your average mystic researcher—but she was terrific at both.

She turned and smiled before giving a stretch. I looked away; she always made me feel guilty; she was, after all, minding her own business and didn't need her boss checking her out. When she finished stretching, she came over and seemed to notice my state for the first time; worry lined her face.

"Zev, what the fuck?" (Remember, nice Jewish girl.) I shrugged and moved around her to see what she was working on. There were two books on her desk; one was an old text on the relationship between water and angels, which was straightforward in my opinion, and exactly what I had expected. The other was some bizarre science book on the behavior of molecules and why they interact differently than other compound elements to temperature. That sounded far too complicated to me.

"I was attacked . . . again." I turned back to her; she looked really worried. It was nice to be cared for by someone who didn't want anything in return. " . . . by a zombie." Her face froze as she processed that.

"'You're shitting me, right?"

"Would I lie to you?" I shot back, and fished the weird objects that I had grabbed at the morgue out of my pocket. "I think these might be related; I would like you to see what you can find out about them." She held out her hand—purple nail polish this time, I noted as I handed them to her. "Thanks, Rivkah." I turned to head back out.

"Whoa; hold on Zev—zombie? Like a 'zombie' zombie? Like a walker?" I shot her a look; at this point, she should know better than to rely on pop mythology. Her nose scrunched adorably; she knew what I was about to say.

"Do you think the producers of your show do as much research as you do? The origin of the word *zombi* has very little to do with the diseased apocalypse of the movies; hell, I'm probably not even using the word right. I think the originally zombis were created through poisoning living people with a specific poison that mimicked death and caused obedience. No, this was a corpse, animated by magic, that attempted to kill me. Non-communicable as far as I know." I paused, I was about to go on about how nothing I had ever encountered could reproduce on the scale or scope of what was shown in movies and TV. Some horrible things did spread their curse, sure—but not as quickly or infectiously as did the zombies of pop culture. But on the other hand, merely experiencing the supernatural pushed humans into a life of being embroiled in it. Perhaps the undead condition wasn't infectious, but the overall supernatural nature of the world surely was. I shook off the melancholic thought before it could invade further. "Sounds like an interesting topic to research, doesn't it? I have to run. I need to figure out what's going on before anyone else decides I look like a good place to rest a knife."

Now that I had wound Rivkah up and set her free to do what she did best, I needed to have a meeting with Shanocht. If my hunch was correct, the body of my assailant had been animated using some poor animal's soul, rather than one from a human. Messing with souls would annoy the ghouls, but stealing and working with corpses would enrage them. It was their food supply, after all. It was no wonder Nathan hated them; devouring bodies would put them at odds with one version of the world to come, where people's bodies would heal and they would be resurrected. I didn't believe in that version of the world to come—but it was hard to justify, even to myself, any alliance with such foul and dangerous creatures. I didn't know how much time I had before the police put two and two together and came to find me. The encounter had given me something concrete to go on, though; I knew my nemesis' name, Basken—that would be the thread I pulled on to unravel all of his plans.

I needed to go to the butcher.

CHAPTER V

$\mathcal{E}$ VEN THOUGH MOST people didn't believe in the supernatural, enough people do that you can find businesses catering to the needs of the magic-using community pretty easily. In Austin, you could find any manner of stone, crystal or gemstone at Nature's Treasures near the Hancock center—but if you wanted something more specialized or ritualistic, Ancient Mysteries off of Ben White was your best bet. It was a small storefront set in a strip along the highway; easy to miss if you weren't already looking for it. While I often didn't see eye-to-eye with other mystical traditions, the people at Ancient Mysteries were good folk.

Walking in, I was happy to see Amanda standing behind the counter; I had helped her with a bhoot[39] a couple of years back, and since then she had been a great source of information when I was stumped. When she saw me she gave a smile, which quickly faded. I rarely came by unless I needed help, and I only needed help when there was something terrible happening. I wasn't the only customer in the store, so I decided to wait a few minutes before approaching Amanda. I walked around the shop, seeing what new

---

39 An Indian ghost or spirit.

inventory there was: dozens of books on new age healing, millennial witchcraft and a few guides on natural herbs and medicine; candles with promises to do everything and anything you could think of.

It isn't that I don't think that these things can work; I know they can—my explanation for the reason they worked just used a syntax that was different than the majority of users'. In my opinion, it was all about tapping into the inner divinity present in every being; the fragrances and herbs and rocks just served as a tether connecting your mind and soul to the concepts you were trying to bring forth. I reached down and picked up a small amulet featuring the seal of Solomon, made famous in a copy of Solomon's Key, a questionable source of mysticism and occult formulae. I had seen the circles and symbols used for protection, summoning, and even odder purposes. I put the amulet back on the wall; these were created en masse somewhere, and no intent or willpower was present in their cold pewter forms. I heard the door close behind the other customers as they finally left.

"Hello, Amanda," I said as I walked up to the counter, offering my trademark horribly-not-reassuring smile. From her wry frown, I assumed it had worked its usual charm.

"What do you want, Zev? You never come to make small talk, or to buy something; there's always a . . . " She flapped her arms in the air as if to pantomime something, though I didn't have any idea what she could be trying to signal. " . . . a thing with you." I gave her a look that I hoped conveyed how hurt I was that she didn't consider that I might have come just to visit her. She didn't look like she was buying it.

"Okay, okay; it's nothing personal, Amanda—that's just how I go through life, only touching on people's lives when I need something like that little boy from *The Giving Tree*." I paused and waited for her to stop giggling. She was a sweet lady, but she needed to get out more if she thought my jokes were funny. "Listen, I had a run-in with some sort of . . . occultist." Labels were dangerous, and I didn't want to offend my best contact in the local pagan scene. "I was wondering if I described the ritual knife he was using if you could give your best guess of where he got it, and maybe what it's used for?"

"Okay, I can try; what do you mean, 'run-in?'" I waved the question off; I didn't want to broadcast what had happened too much.

"It had a blade that curved a bit, almost like a small scimitar; it looked like the handle was covered in black leather and tied down with gold thread, and there was a bit of bright red fabric tied to the hilt, almost like a banner or pennant."

"Was it bone, obsidian, or steel?"

"I think steel. It looked like metal, so I assume it was just a normal knife; nothing too exotic."

I watched Amanda mull over the information I had provided her. "No, I'm sorry Zev; it sounds like the sort of thing someone could have bought at any store that sells fancy knives. If it had been made of something special, maybe, but . . . " She shrugged at me. It had been worth a shot, and it could also be worth it to dig a little deeper—but if this 'Lord' Basken found someone asking about him, he may not hesitate to hurt anyone involved, and I couldn't put her in any danger.

I smiled at her and nodded my thanks. "Okay, but if you happen to hear anything, you let me know as soon as you can, okay?" That left my upcoming attempt to contact Shanocht as my only source of leads; desperate times.

Whenever people consider magic, they usually imagine people either waving wands and spouting Latin, or using sophisticated ingredients with different colored candles—the sort of things you could buy at Ancient Mysteries, which is one reason they did so well with the pseudo-occult community. I would love for that to be the sum of my experience, or even a part of it. I made fairly extensive use of various incenses, and I occasionally lit candles when I was trying to woo Sara, but I had personally never used a wand of any sort. No; instead, I was standing at the butcher buying ten pounds of offal. Just like any other business or job, being an operative of the Beit Din requires you to network. Unlike other industries, my networking occasionally involved inhuman forces that many would consider monsters. Hell, I would consider Shanocht a monster.

The butcher looked at me like I was insane; I was buying the guts and parts that he would generally discard or throw away. I was thankful for the current food culture; bespoke and unique shops were opening everywhere, and this had given rise to an honest-to-god butcher in town. Not a kosher butcher, of course—but I didn't need kosher for what I was doing now. I could tell the butcher was staring at my kippah[40], wondering if this was some crazy thing that Jews do. My suit—complete with tallits katan[41] and tie—didn't help, of course; I couldn't tell him why I actually needed his trash meat. *"Excuse me, sir, I need your finest trash meat to give to a horrible hyena monster that hides during the day and feasts upon corpses in the night!"* That probably wouldn't go over so well. I paid my money, making sure to keep the receipt, and placed the meats in a cooler in my back seat. I was ready to go.

Shanocht traveled throughout the cemeteries of Austin and its small surrounding towns, but during the fall I could usually find him south. I had never asked why; my personal theory was that with all the students coming back to the college town to attend Texas State, the cemeteries would be quiet and peaceful. People traveled during the summer to visit towns like San Marcos, and they took the opportunity to visit their dearly departed during the natural flow of vacationing in the United States. Now that school was back in session, while the city was fuller than ever, the cemetery was emptier.

The drive to San Marcos was no big deal, and I passed Buda and Kyle with no issue before taking a side road towards one of San Marcos' larger cemeteries. While I could never condone what Shanocht is, we had an agreement: he stayed away from Jewish cemeteries, and he fed me information to which no human could have access—and I let him live. He wouldn't come out until night, and there was,

---

40 A small hat worn by Jews, also known as a yarmulke

41 "Small Tallit" An undershirt with frills that stick out from beneath the overshirt

of course, a chance I was at the wrong cemetery—but I had to choose one and hope I was right. I parked and retrieved the cooler, a bouquet of flowers, and a long butterfly knife which I hid in my coat's inner pocket. I had an agreement with Shanocht, but it never paid to be unprepared, and I was getting a little sick of being ambushed. Texas was never really cold, but this late in the year, things were at least cooler. The day was overcast, muting the colors of the leaves that were still on trees. Most plants lifted towards the sky like skeletal fingers, bereft of any flesh or foliage. The cool air was always welcome, though it did make me yearn for a bowl of my mother's chicken soup.

Inside the cemetery, I walked around for a while, looking at each grave and offering a quick prayer. A part of my mind railed against me; I was about to cordially discuss things with a creature that was actively defiling these graves; what right did I have to say blessings for any of these poor people? The intricacies of Jewish law have always been an interesting subject to me. On one hand, there were 613 mitzvot[42]—or rules—that one needed to follow. But the Talmud argued over these, and the sages argued over the Talmud. A common question in yeshiva had been, "What did Rashi[43] say?"—the thought being that if there was something you didn't understand, well, certainly Rashi did . . . but no, Rashi didn't always have a black-and-white answer. I had studied the Zohar[44], the Talmud, and the Torah; I had

42 A rule or law, sometimes translated as good deed.

43 Rabbi Shlomo Yitzchaki, a major commentator on Talmud and Torah, 1040-1105

44 Book of Splendor, major work of Kabbalistic teachings.

spent countless hours pouring over esoteric texts and arguments and legends—but sometimes, things were still not as clear to me as they were to Nathan.

I had a few minutes of sunlight left, and likely a couple of hours before Shanocht stuck his head out of whatever hidey-hole he was using. I set the flowers on a nearby grave and then sat on a bench overlooking the tombs. The ghoul would already know I was present; ghouls had noses capable of tracking carrion and death from miles away. Shanocht had once told me I smelled like a Shinto priest, all incense and tea. There was very little left for me to do but wait.

I don't mind waiting. I closed my eyes and let my mind wander for a few moments, concentrating on my breathing. I hadn't had a chance to meditate and clear my mind for a few days now, and it felt good to return to the rhythm of my own body and mind. After several minutes of just breathing, I allowed my thoughts to turn towards visualization. I imagined the Tetragrammaton[45], the four letters that made up our name for HaShem, before me as white fire on a backdrop of black flames. Considering each letter in turn, I contemplated the visual representation of each. It was an exercise I had learned in Yeshiva, and one I had repeated countless times. It would be hyperbole to say that I discovered something new every time, but it would also be false to say that I had drawn all the wisdom I could from enacting this particular ritual. The Jewish faith frowns on rote behavior; each moment needed to be purposeful, full of meaning—it was one reason we read prayers we had long ago memorized from a siddur. I realized my

---

45 The four letter name of G-d. Yod, Hey, Vav, Hey.

mind had wandered away from the Tetragrammaton, and I gently redirected myself to the second letter of the name—hey—and began to contemplate its meaning.

What must have been a few hours later, I was still on the second letter when I felt eyes on me and could smell the stink of mold and stagnation. Slowly I brought myself out of the meditative state, not opening my eyes yet; I kept my breath even and slow. Panicking would set off most creatures, triggering their feral instincts to hunt and kill. Even after all of these times over the years interacting with it, the presence of the ghoul set me on edge.

"Hello, Shanocht." I kept my voice completely neutral. I could hear it shuffling forward to grab the handle of the cooler I had brought. "Yes, that is for you." Slowly I opened my eyes to view the creature before me. Some believed ghouls had once been human, warped by their devouring of dead human flesh. I didn't think that; ghouls were a race unto themselves, existing like parasites, capable of slipping into even the most well-built necropolis to devour human dead. Their only saving grace was that they didn't breed like rats—but they could also survive for centuries if rumors were true. I didn't know how old Shanocht was, but I doubted it was very old. I suspected an older, more experienced ghoul wouldn't have stuck to our agreement.

The creature standing before me looked mostly human, but was emaciated, like a caricature from a cartoon. Everything about it made it look like someone had stretched it out on the rack; its skin was thin enough that I could see black veins and muscles working just underneath. The worst part was Shanocht's face; it was almost canid, sporting yellowish eyes and a mouth full of hyena-like teeth designed for tearing apart flesh and cracking bones. It looked malicious, like it was planning on tearing into some still-living flesh—but as our eyes met, it winced and looked away, immediately adopting a more submissive posture. Being scary to monsters wasn't necessarily a bad thing, and it had been well-earned. I wondered, as it approached, if it had planned on trying to just kill me and do away with the threat. It would have failed; maybe it knew that. As it dragged the cooler backward towards the open door of a mausoleum, I followed behind; it wouldn't do to have this conversation out in the open, after all.

When I walked into the crypt, Shanocht was already pulling open the cooler to get at the meat inside. If I hadn't held conversations with it before, I would doubt it had the intelligence for real thought. I sat on a bit of stonework and tried to block out the squelching noises coming from my host. I was about to interrupt it when it suddenly looked up at me. Its yellow eyes held fear and greed—but mostly fear.

"This isn't a social visit, Shanocht; I need information."

"I am sorry, Wolf." Its voice sounded like a fish covered in barbed-wire, swimming through a chalkboard tunnel.

I shook my head. "Not interested; what I am interested in is if someone other than ghouls have been grave-robbing—probably up in Tennessee, but I would guess throughout north Texas, too."

"There are always grave robbers, Wolf; your kind

love breaking your own taboos—rings from the wealthy, bodies for study, sometimes just for fun and thrill." Shanocht snorted, its muzzle dripping with gore.

"This would be far a more ritualized version—someone trying to raise the dead; hell, someone doing it. Even if you don't know anything, I would ask you to check sources, see what you hear from your brethren; I'll have more fresh meat for you when you return, to make it worth your while."

Shanocht smiled at that and nodded, reaching into the cooler to lift an intestine and begin chewing on it. "Very kind Wolf, but this . . . " He gestured to his mouth and the cooler of offal. " . . . is not what I apologize for; I apologize for this." Suddenly hands grabbed me from behind, pulling me back, and then down. All around me was darkness and dirt; I could smell that moldy acrid stench that always accompanied Shanocht. The sides of the tunnel I was being dragged through were too small for me, and rocks and roots scratched and tore at me. It was all I could do to remember to breathe. I realized what was happening—Shanocht had sold me out to some more powerful ghoul. The things traveled underground in long tunnels like grubs or ants, connecting cities and cemeteries. While they were lone scavengers as far as I could tell, they still had a massive network of these communal tunnels—and now I was being dragged backward through one of these tunnels at incredible speed.

Just a few minutes and it was over; the tunnel gave way to a room, and I was slammed back into a chair and held by two strong ghoulish hands. I tried to take in my surroundings while I caught my breath. A single naked lightbulb dangled directly above me, illuminating what looked like an unused boiler room—the sort of place one might find on Elm Street. In one corner there was a small staircase that probably led to an empty house. I couldn't make out much more; I assumed from the hands on my shoulders that there were two ghouls behind me, but I was more preoccupied with what was in front of me.

"Wolf is a presumptuous name for prey." The voice—a lazy rasp like a chef halfheartedly sharpening a knife—came from a shape just outside of the circle of light. The shadow of a distressingly tall ghoul, nearly eight feet tall, stepped into the light. The ghoul shared the same stretched-out frame and translucent skin, but instead of rags stolen from human dead, this ghoul was dressed in an immaculate white suit, and a small tarnished silver crown rested on his brow. "Allow me to introduce myself, little Jew; I am Baalrachius, the king of ghouls."

From what I had studied, Baalrachius was ancient—a being that had once stalked the tombs of Sumeria. He had seen history, survived history, and flourished. There were plenty of genuinely ancient monsters in the world; usually, they didn't concern themselves with the day-to-day actions of humans. After thousands of years, even the worship of lesser beings probably became boring. Baalrachius was different. I didn't know if he was the being once worshiped as Baal, but it wouldn't surprise me. Baalrachius paced in front of me now, one of the most dangerous individual creatures in the country. I didn't bow my head to him; I wouldn't submit or be docile to the monster. He had subjugated people—murdered plenty—and on top of all of that, he had hurt my friend.

"I thought you went back north to New York after you crippled Father Enrique," I said. Baalrachius stopped his pacing and turned towards me, leaning down to put his face near mine. His breath reeked of decay, and his eyes were solid white—no iris, no pupils. His smile was cruel and predatory.

"Enrique was hunting my people, and he felt his young faith guaranteed him safety from retribution. He was wrong. Now, little Wolf, Shanocht tells me you are the most powerful magician in the south, which means you are the most likely suspect for my current ills." He practically spat the word magician out at me, and I remembered that Shanocht had once told me that the King of Ghouls despised practitioners of any mystical tradition. He felt that we were all charlatans, not fit share in the power of creatures like him. I had pressed to find out more; after all, if Shanocht could use any form of magical power, I had never seen it. It would be beyond useful to know if ghouls could use spellwork. Generally speaking—as far as I could tell, anyway—things could either use magic or were magic; not both. But then again, the sheydim completely ignored that rule. If the thing in front of me was some sort of a practitioner, he would have had millennia to study and grow in power. I struggled against the hands that were holding me down in the chair, but they were unrelenting; ghouls possessed a strength that seemed counter to their thin frames.

I looked back to Baalrachius' face, still only inches away from my own. "I wouldn't call myself a magician—or powerful, for that matter, Baal." I observed his face, but he didn't seem to be irritated by my use of the shorter version of his name, which was a good start. "I happen to know a few tricks that I have used to protect my kind, but that's it; I certainly haven't been hunting ghouls, which Shanocht should have also told you." True, for the most part—I certainly didn't consider myself a magician or sorcerer, even if I did have some nice juju up my sleeves.

Baalrachius' lips curled back into a wicked snarl of a smile. "I didn't say you were hunting my people; I said that you were causing problems. You are the one that is causing the dead to become restless in this part of the world, hmm? From Tennessee all the way down through Mexico, our food is fighting back—and would you say this is not your doing?" The part of me that was hoping to find answers here was disappointed. If Baalrachius thought I was the culprit that was bringing the dead back to life, then the ghouls were even more clueless than I was. Now I just needed to survive this encounter with my spine intact.

"No, it is not my doing; necromancy is forbidden in my tradition Baal. The person doing this has targeted me—I was attacked, stabbed; I've actively been working to identify and stop the people who have been doing this. Believe it or not, we're on the same side on this one." I was rambling a bit, but hopefully suggesting that my actions were serving his interest would encourage him to give me some leniency.

Baalrachius wrenched my tie to the side and ripped open my shirt, exposing my poor, belabored stitches. He glanced at my face before smiling at me again and using two of his long clawed fingers to rip open the stitches on my shoulder. He pushed a finger into the wound, digging around in my shoulder before withdrawing his finger and licking it clean. He may have been talking during this; I couldn't hear him over my own panicked screams. It was all I could do to pant and swallow my fear. With my blood in the air, I could hear the ghouls holding me down licking their lips. Baalrachius shrugged, standing up straight and turning his back to me.

"It may be true; it may not be—you do not taste like a liar, little Wolf, but you don't taste innocent either. I can smell the rot of undeath on you; maybe you were attacked, or maybe you are trying to save your own skin." He waved dismissively. "It will be easier to kill you now, and if you are telling the truth, I can deal with whoever is left over. If you are lying, I deal with the problem here and now. Goodbye, little Wolf." With that dismissal he walked to a door on the far side of the room and exited, waving a hand to signal his conclusion of the interview before the door slammed closed, leaving me alone with the two ravenous ghouls at my shoulders.

Nothing moved for a moment; the creatures holding me were probably making sure their king was gone before making a move to devour me alive. I didn't want to give them the time to make decisions or a move. Slowly, as if I was only reaching up to touch the wound that Baalrachius had ripped open, I reached into my coat and gripped my knife. Thank HaShem I had the foresight to bring it with me. I took two deep breaths, readying myself for action and focusing my mind away from the pain in my shoulder.

I flipped the knife open with practiced ease, slashing through the fingers of the ghoul on my right and pushing forward as soon as I had; judging based on standard ghoul height and where their hands were, I made a guess and turned the knife in my hand to slash across the leftmost ghoul's throat. Pushing back against the chair, I put some distance between myself and the two ghouls. I didn't need to worry; they had not been prepared to fight.

The ghoul whose neck I had slashed was slowly sinking to its knees, attempting to staunch the cascade of black ichor that was pouring from its throat; the other held its hand close to its chest, glaring at me with an intense hatred bordering on madness. Realizing that his compatriot was going to die, the injured ghoul surged forward with a screech. I may be injured, but I wasn't going to keep letting things kick my ass. I dodged under the creature's attack and swung upwards, slashing its armpit before aiming a kick at its knee. I was rewarded by the crunch of bone going the wrong way, and as it fell back, I followed up with another slash to the eyes. Once again, I was rewarded as the thing screamed in a panicked pain and crawled away from me. Blinded and hurt, the ghouls had underestimated me, and the two creatures were now paying with their lives. I stepped forward and slit the feral creature's throat—

no sense in letting it suffer and bleed out. Murder is a cardinal sin, and yet protecting one's own life was a commandment; I wasn't sure Baalrachius would accept that explanation—would a thing like that care that its minions had died? Would it accept that these things happened? Or would I find myself broken and left on the floor, like my friend Father Enrique?

I stepped past the body of the ghoul as it convulsed in its death rattles. I wasn't worried about evidence; some creature would be along shortly to devour the corpses. I could only hope it wouldn't be ghouls that discovered bodies. I dashed for the ladder leading to the hatch, and quickly made it up and out into a brisk night. I closed the hatch behind me and headed out into the open air. I was in another cemetery; I glanced back at the hatch before taking a quick jog out of the graveyard. Ghouls could still chase me—they could attack me wherever they wanted to, really—but it would be rare for them to leave the protection of their home turf. I was still in San Marcos, which was a relief; I could easily call an Uber and get back to my car without too many problems. I needed to get back to Austin. I had spent the last few days getting ambushed and attacked, and I needed to turn things around and go on the offensive.

CHAPTER VI

J T WAS LATE, and I needed to get back to Sara before she started to panic. It wasn't the most natural thing in the world, lying to friends and family about what you did every day—made harder when the worlds collided, like when Rivkah stopped by to drop off haunted statues while my mother way visiting, or when a cultist stabbed me in my home and I had to stay with Sara. I formulated my excuse as I drove back to Austin. My cover job was a fantastic smoke screen when I was living by myself. It was dull enough that no one ever really wanted to know more, giving me a comfortable lie to remember; when I was out late, well, that wasn't anything special—an event, tutoring, a special prayer session, almost any explanation worked because of the intricacies of an organized religion with so much ritual and community. Hardly anyone knew everything that was going on at a synagogue at any given time. Of course, my mother was disappointed that my career wasn't more impressive; she had thought I would be a rabbi once, and then a great general—some sort of career-heavy leader—but as far as she was concerned, I was happy, and I made enough money that she couldn't complain too much.

When I walked in, I braced for impact from Tooth, who launched himself at my knees in a desperate bid to lick at me. The round creature heaved and gasped, his entire butt wiggling with the force of his wags. It's good for the soul when something loves you so much that it can't contain it. Dogs were good for the soul.

"There you are! Don't tell me you went to work in your condition!" Yup, that's what I was waiting for.

"Had to; we had an event tonight and Dennis is on vacation, so I didn't have a choice." I had been lying so long about my life that it was second nature—I knew all my fake coworkers' habits and schedules, where they went, what their family lives were like. I didn't have to think about my responses, and after all this time, I didn't feel guilty. "But you're right, I busted my stitches again; I was hoping you could help me out."

Seeing my torn shirt and the wound in my shoulder, Sara squealed; she was a big softy, and with that she dropped all of her anger to come and baby me once again. It was a nice feeling, and could be a sweet life in theory. Of course, it couldn't be my life. It wasn't that the Beit Din forbade marrying, but how could you keep it a secret from your spouse? How could you keep it a secret from someone you lived with—and even if you could, even if you did for a time, as soon as she found out that I had lied to her for years, well—that would be the end of any positive relationship I had.

"How the hell did you do that, Ze'ev Kaplan?" Sara asked as she moved forward and examined the wound. "What kind of event causes you to bust your stitches—did you wrestle with a bar mitzvah student, or something?"

"Last time, I swear." I leaned against the toilet as Sara stitched me back up. Beneath me, her dog continuously licked my foot. "Your dog is weird. He knows my foot isn't chicken, right?" I smiled up at her, trying to keep positive through the pain and the frustrating knowledge that every time this wound opened, the scar it would leave was getting more and more noticeable.

"He isn't weird. He's sweet, and you could learn a thing or two from him," Sara said.

I shot her a look. "You want me to lick your feet? Okay, I take it back; you're the weird one."

Sara laughed at that; she was probably a bit more adventurous than I was. While I enjoyed a lot of her ideas, I didn't think I was going to pick up licking toes any time soon. "When you finish this, I think a shower and then bed sounds wonderful . . . do you want to join me for evening prayers?" I didn't ask her that very often; only when I was stressed. I felt like the community is at the heart of my faith as a Jew, and saying prayers with another person—especially one you love—is a powerful expression of that faith.

She scrunched her nose at me and shook her head. I didn't mind. I knew she would say no when I asked. It was the only real ruffle in my relationship with Sara. Usually, I didn't mind too much. I did love her, after all; the question became more pertinent when I considered the long-term ramifications of our relationship. Could I marry a woman who didn't share my faith, and raise kids? What about my secret life, and the lies I had to tell—not to even mention the lies I had already told. It was less than ideal, and one day, I would have to deal with all of these issues. But for now, I felt I could just breathe, relax, and leave those problems for the future.

Despite not wanting to join me for a shower or prayers, Sara did want to make sure she got to spend some time with me in the bedroom. As always, she was insatiable; tonight, she took charge, pushing me down and riding me to her satisfaction, which left me slightly bruised—spent, but happy. I watched her sleeping for a moment, but my mind was too busy to go to sleep just yet. I had been in plenty of dangerous situations, both mundane and supernatural. I had served in the IDF's special services, and it was hard to get more dangerous than that—but things like this, happening in my home city—hell, in my home . . . that was different. That wasn't endangering just me, or soldiers; that was endangering people like Sara and Rivkah—hell, even Tooth probably wasn't safe.

I stepped out onto the balcony of Sara's home, partly just watching the night, partly doing my best to make sure no surprises were lurking just outside. As I've said, I was done getting ambushed by these cretins. Baalrachius had called me a powerful practitioner, and while I wouldn't necessarily have called myself that, the fact of the matter was, I was a big fish in a small pond. Especially in the American South, I didn't have that much competition. I would pull out the stops, and show 'Basken' that not even wizards could get away with anything they wanted to—not while I was still alive, anyway. In the morning, I would check back in with Rivkah and begin hunting down this cult.

Rivkah assaulted me as soon as I crossed the threshold of our lab.

"So, these things are disgusting," Rivkah very nearly shouted, nearly bouncing with her excitement; I looked away from my diminutive assistant so that I wouldn't just be staring down her shirt as she bounced and moved across the lab towards her workstation, pulling the goggles from her head. I followed after her. "Zev, you don't understand how cool these things are—what they could mean for science!"

I shot her a look, doing my best to appear as a disapproving mentor. "The scientific community hasn't exactly been our friend in the past." I didn't hate science; I loved science, and I firmly believed that when science contradicted religion, we had to go back and look at the words of faith and try to reinterpret them—that our understanding was flawed, rather than the faith. But the fact did remain that when there was something science couldn't explain, it was far more likely for the community to cry fraud and try to discredit those who had brought the information forward. I didn't want to see Rivkah on the receiving end of that kind of attention.

If she heard me at all, she didn't react; she was far too busy grabbing my arm to drag me along faster. She stopped at her desk and gestured to her microscope proudly, like a mother showing off her child's first steps. I looked at her patiently; sometimes Rivkah forgot that not everyone understood how to use her toys. She rolled her eyes at me and moved to look through the microscope herself. "The little things you brought me—at first I thought they were dead maggots, right?" I shuddered, but her supposition made sense, seeing as they had come out of the mouth of a corpse. I wasn't the biggest fan of bugs; lots of horrible things made use of insects, and I didn't think I would ever come to terms with the things.

When she moved aside, I looked through the microscope, not sure to what I would be treated. The thing in the view looked an awful lot like a maggot, but not one made out of flesh; a snarling human face with mandibles was visible on the small thing. I peered at it, horrified by how disgusting it looked and trying to discern out of what it could be made. Suddenly it writhed under the light, turning to look at me, its mandibles clacking. I like to think that I leaped back, cool, calm and ready to act; the reality was, I probably stumbled away shrieking a little (if Rivkah's face was anything to go by). I glared at her from where I landed.

"It moved, right? Here's the crazy part: it's made of wood, it's a little wooden carving, and it moves!" Rivkah helped me to my feet, going into mile-a-minute explanation-mode as she tended to do whenever she found something fascinating. "It isn't alive, not really; as far as I can tell, things like this were carved and then some demon or soul was trapped inside, held by the magic of whoever made them." I looked at her broadly-grinning face as she continued to expound on the thermodynamic properties of possessed wood.

"I'm sorry, Rivkah—did you just tell me that there is a demon trapped in each of these little maggot carvings?" She stopped midsentence, irritation at my interruption written across her face.

"Yes; I mean, in theory—I think so? I can't see that sort of thing, and there aren't really tests; I figured you would be a better judge of that." I nodded and pulled the carving off her microscope, so that I could let it rest in my hand while I contemplated it. A demonic spirit or entity was a severe problem.

"And you said that it's held in there by the magic of whoever bound it?"

"Supposition, Zev—but I think so? I couldn't find a lot on this in the books; this isn't Jewish magic, obviously; it's . . . "

"Treif." Treif wasn't exactly right—it meant that food was not Kosher, not fit for consumption by Jews—but in a pinch it worked here, too; necromancy was strictly forbidden in the Jewish tradition, a bit more severe than shellfish, and I had fallen into the habit of trying to explain magic to new initiates in terms of Treif and kosher. It had stuck in our vernacular.

I moved to a small area in the lab that was mostly empty—other than a meditation pillow and a small bookshelf—and keeping my eyes on the sliver of wood in my palm, I sank onto the cushion and began to push myself towards a meditative state. Rivkah had seen me do this often enough that she stopped trying to educate me on science that was frankly way above my head. She moved to sit and watch over me.

Contrary to popular belief, you didn't need complete silence, darkness, or Enya music to meditate successfully; I find most meditative tools to be distracting, anyway—and my best meditations were done during morning prayers. I simply let go of my preconceived ideas of what was happening, becoming aware of my body and what each moment in time was telling me on its own. After a few moments of becoming acclimated to this way of thinking and observing the world, I turned my attention outward towards the carving in my hand.

The meditative state was the most frequently-used tool in my arsenal, and I employed it before using anything that would resemble miracles or magic, other than true pronunciations; it heightened my focus and awareness. Of course, no matter how hard I looked with human eyes, I wouldn't be able to see souls. I kept the image of the carving in my mind, as I closed my eyes and focused my full concentration on the image in my mind.

Slowly, I could see something pulse from within the shape of the carving—a dull greenish light that seemed to throb like a luminescent heartbeat. It wasn't a demon, or sheyd; the light that pulsed was entirely human. The monsters had trapped human souls within these diminutive totems. I would need to exorcise and cleanse each of the totems to free the victims of this sorcery—but there, behind the throbbing energy of the dybbuk, I could sense something else: an ethereal smear of energy that almost resembled greasy smoke. I could smell it now, like the oil pan from a fryer that hadn't been changed in months. The rancid smell almost made me gag, which quickly brought me out of my meditative state.

I opened my eyes to see Rivkah standing over me, mouth agape. In my hand, the maggot carving was smoldering, giving off the same smoke I saw in my vision without being consumed. I smiled grimly. "That's their magic, their connection to this thing; I can follow it straight to the source." Slowly the smoke dissipated; no longer called into being by my willpower, it was still there—intangible, but traceable. I stood suddenly and made a beeline for another shelf; this one was stocked with all the bits and ends you would expect to see in an alchemist's shop. I set the sliver of wood on a nearby table, while I fetched various dried plants and began bundling them up. It was nothing special—mostly different herbs connected with protection and cleansing, with a few doses of psilocybe cubensis, my old friend magic mushrooms. I doubt Nathan would be thrilled at my use of hallucinogens, but as an aid to certain wondrous actions, they were indispensable. At least Rivkah never judged. I put the blend into a tea kettle and then moved it to a single burner we kept here. Setting the kettle down, I glanced at Rivkah.

"So, once I drink this, I'm going to need you to watch over me."

"While you're tripping balls?" Well, she wasn't always the most eloquent.

"Essentially." I explained. "The mushrooms are going to help me take a—well, yes, a trip. I'll find and hopefully deal with this cult problem in one fell swoop, but while I'm out-of-it I'm going to be pretty much defenseless."

"Should I grab the shotgun?" Rivkah wasn't what I would call a violent person—despite her obsession with music that sounded like angry cats screaming at one another—but I had taken her to the shooting range a few times; I wanted my assistant to be able to defend herself. Turns out, now she could protect me, too. What I was about to attempt was incredibly dangerous—and wildly unpredictable—but I needed to get an edge; otherwise, I would be on the run for the rest of my very short life.

My tea tasted disgusting. Every time I made a tea like this, I always promised I would add some mint, lemon, or honey—and I always forgot. There was something about lives, souls, and my family being on the line that made me rush, and forget basic steps like making my tea drinkable. Rivkah was losing her shit—clutching her stomach and laughing at the faces I was making as I drank down my concoction. Good flavor wasn't a requirement to work wonders, but it helped.

"If you can stop laughing at me—your boss—for a moment, make a note to add some lemon next time." I finished the rest of the tea in a few gulps, and then returned to the meditation pillow to take a seat. Using mind-expanding drugs was dangerous all by its lonesome, even before I started adding in hazardous activities. I wasn't one to shirk danger, but what I had planned was a triple threat: fry my brains with drugs, walk through the dreams of my enemies and then confront them. "So, if I start foaming at the mouth, if cuts start appearing on my body or I just keel over—burn some sage and make sure I don't swallow my tongue, or anything."

With her agreement not to willfully let me die, I once again settled and began concentrating on my breath. I had messed around with acid and drugs a bit after my time in the military, but I was no expert. I sometimes worried that I would not add enough of a given substance, and I wouldn't achieve the results I needed—or that I would macro-dose myself and have an adverse reaction to the drugs. For a few moments this time, I thought I had done the former. My breath seemed even, my heartbeat was calm; everything seemed perfectly natural. I could feel the air curling into my lungs, filling me with raw energy—and as it escaped my lips on the exhale it was scorched, with smoke and flames licking from my mouth. With my eyes closed, I watched the flames that escaped my body slip into the air, transforming into snakes that watched me carefully before slithering into the sky.

After a moment, I realized I didn't need to worry about having under-dosed myself, and mentally pushed the hallucinations away. I couldn't squash them entirely, but I didn't need them distracting me from my current goal. I opened my hand, and after a moment, I felt Rivkah drop the tiny maggot carving into my waiting palm. Focusing my mind's eye, I quickly found the greasy smoke that came off of the totem. The smoke coalesced in thick rings, now that I was viewing it through the lens of some chemical help. With one last deep breath, I pushed up and out of myself, stepping away from my meditating form to follow the trail of the magic tying this totem to my antagonist.

CHAPTER VII

THERE IS AN old proverb that a dream left uninterpreted was like a gift left unopened—but usually a story was read along with the same proverb.

A woman came to the rabbi and asked him to interpret a dream. Upon listening to the young woman's dream, the rabbi said, 'You are going to have a son,' and the woman went home, and within the year she gave birth to a son. Two years later, she once again returned to the rabbi with a dream that needed deciphering. Once again, the rabbi listened, and when she was finished, he smiled and told her, 'You are going to have a daughter.' Sure enough, within a few months the woman was with child—a daughter this time. A third time the woman came, but the rabbi was traveling—so his students listened to her dreams, and a student told her, 'Your husband is going to die.' When the rabbi learned of this, he rebuked his students, saying that by interpreting the dream in this manner they were responsible for the death of the husband.

Dreams exist in a purely subjective realm, where we are more in tune with the ability to exert control over the world around us. Our thoughts and ideas bleed into reality from our dreams, but within the dreams themselves, the impossible is always ordinary. Dreamwalking is one of the most dangerous things I could do. From my limited understanding, there were shamanistic traditions that had a much safer time of it—or at least, there were shaman who were skilled enough in walking through dreams that to them it was second nature.

Because my thoughts were bent towards necromancers and ghouls, my dreamscape was filled with the dead. A necropolis rose around me, things with limbs far too long to be human shuffling within the shadows just out of sight. I saw the flash of Baalrachius' white suit in every glint of light. Towering above me, like a skyscraper rising from behind the tombs and buildings around me was a figure dressed in robes, the face hidden in the shadows of its hood. Its arms outstretched above it, dominating the skyline, in one hand, the figure, a stand-in for the necromancer Basken I assumed, clutched a curved sacrificial knife. Well, Basken *was* looming over my every thought.

I did my best to ignore the macabre landscape and the phantoms that flitted through the shadows. The greasy smoke hung in the air before me; I reached out and grabbed it, the smoke transforming into a black rope, suspended in air. So far, so good—but I didn't want to press my luck too much, so I began following the trail, half-pulling myself, half-walking. I mostly knew what I was looking for, and I knew what I should probably avoid—but the truth was that my quarry likely had the dead on his brain, too.

Humans are not the only creatures that can walk

through dreams; I have encountered sheydim here—creatures that were created during the dusk of the first Shabbot, unfinished, and commonly referred to as demons, though they were often more like faerie than like the conventional idea of demons. Things that I called devils also stalked the dreams of man. It wasn't an accurate term; they certainly weren't the horned creatures from Christian mythology. What I called devils were creatures that didn't fit easily into other categories: spiritual beings from other faiths, magical creatures with no basis in folklore, and nightmares made of madness that had torn themselves from another reality to this one.

I wasn't an expert on dreams—even as I pulled myself through the twisted landscape of my recent nightmares—but I have always felt that dreams were a world of their own; perhaps a buffer between the world we currently live in and other realms that existed out there. It certainly seemed a more common ground for all the unnatural things in existence. There was a story—though I couldn't remember where I originally read it—that HaShem had left one corner of creation unfinished. HaShem told the administrating angels, 'Let any who feel they can better create, do so here." This unfinished bit could have been an explanation for the lifeless deserts, but this story was used as an explanation for anything that seemed difficult to attribute to HaShem. I didn't buy that theory; I was a follower of the nondual philosophy.

Here and there as I followed the black rope through strange vistas, I could see things that looked like half-remembered insects dissolving into cephalopods, watching me as I passed. I did my best not to notice them. In this place where the mind was the same as matter, giving the monsters a second thought gave them that much more mass and power.

I had just finished swimming through an underwater kingdom—with mushrooms that radiated thousands of bright red lights dotting the ceiling—when I realized that I recognized my current surroundings. The sun was setting over an expansive plain; dry and dead cotton fields surrounded me as far as I could see in any direction. I realized I had made a miscalculation; I had entered my dreams far too quickly after having the nightmare. There was no chance that I could escape without confronting it here. Sure enough, as I finished scanning the horizon and turned back to face my path, the dilapidated farmhouse loomed ahead of me, the rope of smoke and energy stretching through the doors and into the shadows. It wasn't that the dream world was forcing me to face my fears in some test to see if I was worthy; no, the creation of this place was entirely my own doing.

That didn't make it less horrifying—or less deadly. I moved slowly, entirely in control of my own body this time; at least here and now I had some say over what my body did. I shivered, feeling a cold wind blowing from inside those doors, the smell of death and musk of decay heavy in the air. Nothing felt less real than the day I was being forced to relive, no one sensation dulled by time's passing or overexposure to the memory. I could feel my stomach dropping into my bowels, urging me to turn and run. Surely this cult problem could solve itself, and perhaps even death would be preferable to walking through those doors yet again. I knew that wasn't true—issues didn't solve themselves, and evil left alone only grew stronger.

I walked through the doors and into the shadows of the barn. It was not as empty here, in dreams, as it had been in reality. All around me, strung from the walls, impaled on spikes and splayed open with tools of torture were friends and allies, people I had come to know and had loved through the long years since my childhood. Nathan hung from the ceiling, disemboweled, his entrails dripping to the floor underneath him. My mother's head sat on a table, face frozen in a silent scream, her body nowhere to be found. I shut my eyes, knowing full-well that it was pointless—that I would be able to see them even with my eyes tightly closed. In one corner Sara and Rivkah were crucified near one another, their bodies bruised and abused from the kind of violence only monsters could enjoy. Scattered throughout the building were other friends: there was Joe-Jack, body broken with a meat tenderizer; there was Detective Barman, each limb cut from his body and strewn into a pile.

I could feel my bile rising, tears coming to my eyes; I knew that none of this was real—all of these people were alive and well. My nightmares were born from the idea that my loved ones would suffer. I always worried that the things I hunted and from which I worked to protect the world would discover me, and move not against me but against the people I loved. If I was honest with myself, being attacked in my home was almost a relief, because it meant that my enemies were coming directly for me. I shook my head and walked forward, past the frozen tableau of torture, keeping one hand loosely on my guiding rope—this madness was only the first part of the nightmare, the rest waiting for me out the back door.

Outside, standing just to the left of the door, was a man—breathtakingly beautiful, wearing luminous robes. He stood a full head taller than me, and there was a condescending smile frozen on his perfect lips. His head was topped with fiery red hair that curled and seemed to dance even when frozen in time, looking like actual flames. He had been here, but not like this; in reality, the beautiful man—Domah—had been broken and bloody, near death. Behind me on the other side of the door would be the thing that had killed the beautiful man, a creature of madness and hatred manifested. It had also been near-death, keening out its last sanity, rending screams of pain. Would it be in pristine condition, like the man I saw now?

My answer came before I could turn around; something shifted behind me, and I could hear it breathing—a wheezing, gasping breath coming out of dozens of mouths, each one hungry to tear flesh from bones. Something brushed against my leg, and I ran.

I don't know how long I ran. I couldn't look back, and until I had to I couldn't stop. My lungs were burning, my legs aching; I fell to my knees, one hand hanging on to the rope, forcing me to nearly dangle while I tried to catch my breath. As I sucked in whatever passed for air in this place, I realized one of the shadows from my surroundings had broken off and approached me—a shadow that I recognized.

"Baladan." I acknowledged the diminutive humanoid before me, in a now-ragged voice. Baladan was a minor imp, serving in the courts of the sheydim as something of a messenger and jester. His name literally translated as 'Not a Man,' although I didn't know who would mistake this tiny creature for a man. He looked mostly like a Pomeranian, with monkey feet and long, reptilian claws for hands. It was often difficult to tell what he was thinking, behind his canine face. After waiting long enough to make me wonder if he was a hallucination, too, he tilted his head and spoke in a voice like thousands of spiders walking across glass.

"Sorcerer; little Wolf; big, bad Ze'ez—lost and alone in half-formed land." He danced from one paw to another before he suddenly froze, his ears perking at some squelching noise off in the distance.

"I'm not lost, Baladan; I'm . . . " I shouldn't give him too much. While the sheydim were far from the evil entities portrayed in art, they could be malicious, and Baladin's one-track mind probably hadn't noticed the rope along which I was dragging myself. "I assume you came to deliver a message, and not to drag me off to Ashmandei's[46] court for the sheydim's amusement; I would appreciate it if you would get on with it."

Baladin's muzzle wrinkled in annoyance. He had wanted to play games, not rush through on his errand, and it looked like he was struggling on whether to do his job or not for a few moments, before letting out a long sigh.

"The one you stand against alone; it has been written that he who stands in his way shall have a place in the world to come." That was interesting, but I had no reason to doubt the veracity of the words, just the reason for them. "There are those in the court

---

46 King of the Sheydim, also known as Asmodeus

of my lord, who wish you to know that if you stand against them, you will not see the world to come." Well, that was a mixed message; I needed more details, especially if I was about to get wrapped up in the political plots of the sheydim. As I opened my mouth, Baladin interrupted by opening *his* mouth—giving me a good view of his impossible number of teeth jutting out at impossible angles—and letting out a blood-curdling howl.

I looked around as I heard things stirring in the dark, creatures taking notice; Baladin cackled wildly, but when I looked back, he had disappeared. Of course, he had to make this more difficult than it had to be for me. My break was over; I wasted no more time trying to recover, and resumed pulling myself along the rope that represented the magical connection from the necromancer to the totem. I was close, though I didn't know how long it had taken to get this far—it could have been minutes or hours—but now I could see the faint outline of a house; I could see street signs and addresses. It was a race now—could I reach my destination before those things formed in dreams could reach me?

My arms ached; my lungs felt like they were on fire, but now I could see not just the house, but the terminus of the rope—as it neared the necromancer, it dissolved back into smoke. Through the darkness beginning to close in on me, I could see that my target was alone, and seemed to be in some small room. I pulled myself one last time, letting go of the rope to fling myself at the cultist. This would be the most dangerous part of my parlor trick, but probably the part I was also most comfortable performing.

CHAPTER VIII

IN DREAMS, our connection to the divine is raw, capable of shaping all of reality on a whim. But all things are connected, as I've said—if all things are HaShem, pieces of the divine—then placement doesn't matter too much. The whole universe is one, and my particular part of the one could be anywhere within it. Touching into the divine spark within myself and connecting it to the divine all around me in the dream realm allowed me to slide my position within the universe, from one place to another.

My dream body slid into reality two feet in front of—and above—the cultist whose magic was connected to the totem back in my lab. I carried the momentum I had in the dream with me into the waking world and extended a fist as I fell, landing a punch with a satisfying crunch that sent the man sprawling. I took a moment to take in the room I had landed in, and realized I was in a private home bathroom. Hopefully it was his home, and hopefully he was alone. Otherwise, my entire plan would fall apart and I would find myself more exposed than before. The man—it had to be Basken—had landed in a heap next to the toilet. I couldn't hear anyone coming to investigate, and a quick glance told me the door was unlocked; most likely I was safe for the time being.

The man looked like the sort of guy who would get pulled in by a cult—a little on the scrawny side, with oily skin and unkempt hair. He was the kind of man who had been made to feel powerless throughout a lifetime of not fitting in. He had probably had his brushes with white power websites, and I bet I would be able to find a fedora in his regular wardrobe if I checked. The man looked terrified; even someone who dabbled in magic and the supernatural wasn't used to seeing someone appear from thin air and start throwing punches. Remnants of the dream clung to my body, appearing in the real world like tendrils of distortion, clinging to me. I moved towards the young man, doing my best to look intimidating—not tricky under the circumstance; he started shrieking as soon as I leaned over him.

"Who are you? What do you want?" He put out his hands, flailing and trying to ward me away. This was definitely not the leader of the group—any group; he had the air of a flunky. I reached down and made a grab for his shoulder, but my hand passed right through. I had used up too much of whatever energy allowed me to project myself through the dreams to this man's home. I wasn't all that surprised; while I had never attempted to fight someone while dreamwalking before, I knew that any ability to interact with the world depended on my reserves of will power and stamina, both of which felt stretched thin at the moment.

"Foul spirit!"—still with the shrieking; this guy needed to calm down—"I fear you not!" He began muttering something under his breath; it sounded suspiciously like Latin. Every so often, he would make a bizarre sign with his hands, and it slowly dawned on me that he was attempting to exorcise me. He thought I was a ghost. Even though I wasn't dead, there was a chance that whatever banishing magic he was trying to conjure up would work on me—with the best-case scenario being it sent me back to my own body. I pushed my face directly into his, eye-to-eye. I wondered if he could feel or smell my breath. I could play the ghost card, or . . .

"I am no ghost, you tuchas lekar[47]. I am the man after whom your master is sending you." That interrupted his little incantation; the color drained from his face. Luckily, my bluff worked—he assumed if I wasn't a ghost his little banishing attempt wouldn't work.

"You're the exorcist, the one in Memphis—but I sent . . . "

"Yes, y'all sent a man to kill me—and when he failed, Basken had him killed and raised to try to finish the job. I'm guessing you were the trigger man for that little job, right?"

"I didn't want to kill Yash, but I had to. I didn't have a choice!"

"Murder is never the only choice!" I roared at him. "Certainly not murder and then desecration." It astounded me how quickly he confessed; he was definitely dealing with a guilty conscience. How twisted did one man have to become, before he felt that murder was justified? How much further, before necromancy seemed like an ethical choice? I had

---

47 Yiddish, ass-licker.

expected a more cartoonish evil—or at least someone who basked in their own sin.

"You don't understand; to learn—to become powerful—I have to do what Lord Basken requires. If I don't, then he'll just use me!" That was my way into his head—he feared Basken enough that I might be able to use his guilt and fear to convince him to turn on his master.

"If you continue down this path, you will have a bigger problem than him, and you will have to answer to me. I can find you, no matter where you are, or how you hide—tell me where your master is!" It was hard to be menacing when I couldn't touch him, and talking like a magician from Dungeons and Dragons sounded weird, even to my ears—but I had to make him believe I was all-powerful, that he should fear me more than Basken. It looked like it was working.

"I don't know. No one knows where he lives!"

"Tell me where I can find him, unless you want to share in his fate!" I was practically shouting now, but it came out as barely a whisper; pushing through the dreams and materializing here was taking everything out of me. I needed to finish here, before I was forced to wake up. "Absolve yourself; answer me!" Trembling, the fledgling necromancer nodded.

"We meet at a warehouse in Dallas; it's 1340 Motor Circle . . . please protect me from Basken—you said you wouldn't kill me." I let him beg. I was being pulled back to my body; I closed my eyes and let myself be reeled back.

When I reopened my eyes, I saw Rivkah standing over me looking concerned. I smiled a little, watching relief wash over her face. I stood slowly, shakily, and stretched out. It felt like I had been sitting in that position for days.

"Okay; call the police and put in an anonymous tip—tell them you saw a man at 1500 Technicenter Drive murder an Indian man . . . no other information, just that."

"You found the killers? What were they like? Were they wearing, like, dark robes?"

"There was a huge pit . . . The cultists were mostly half-dressed, probably because there looked like molten stone and metal in the pit—so it was hot, right?"

"Uh-huh?" Rivkah looked entranced at the concept.

"They had a woman in a cage, suspended from a ceiling that they could lower on some sort of winch into the pit; the head cultist was wearing a headdress, and chanting . . . ."

"Ze'ev?" Rivkah suddenly asked, interrupting me.

"Yes?"

"Are you just describing Indiana Jones and the Temple of Doom?" She questioned, now looking irritated.

"Yes," I admitted, grinning. "No robes, no pit; it was just a guy in some blue jeans, making himself some instant ramen. Even I'm somewhat disappointed."

She laughed, flipping me off with a plum-nailed middle finger as she turned to grab the phone.

My guess was that as soon as he saw the cops, it would all come pouring out. Hell, maybe he would admit to everything, and bring the entire cult down without me having to raise another finger. The chances of that happening were pretty slim. I couldn't take the chance that Basken wouldn't stay free and keep coming after me; it seemed like I needed to take a trip to Dallas.

I-35 North was a long stretch of highway; you could take it from the Mexican American border to Minnesota without breaking stride, except for a critical couple of traffic-prone cities. That said, the drive between Austin and Dallas was never a fun one. I put on a playlist of Tom Waits, Portishead, and Bob Dylan, and put the tires to the highway. The worst part of driving in Texas is the monotony—miles upon miles of plains, with nothing but power lines and the occasional ranch house to break up the scenery. Out here in North Texas, there were so many empty places. I reminded myself that hundreds—if not thousands—of people made this trip every single day without incident. The likelihood of something expanding out of those empty places to come for me was slim to none. Knowledge of what was out there, slumbering under the tranquil lakes of Texas, didn't mean that those things had knowledge of me—or that they would even care. I was insignificant to most things; a dagesh[48], easily dismissed by the things that saw into the true alefbet[49] that made up our reality.

That said, understanding that there was a truth underlying reality did make me more noticeable to

---

48 A small dot changing the sound of the Hebrew letter it is combined with

49 The Hebrew alphabet, from the first two letters Alef, Bet

those things under quiet waters. Generally speaking, the magnetism of a human who knows of the supranatural world attracted the attention and presence of said world without either party even being cognizant of it. Even if I were to retire and leave behind the life of an exorcist, these things would still find me; they would still seek me out—but it didn't stop me from day dreaming and wishful thinking.

I plowed through Waco, Hillsboro, and Waxahachie quickly. Just past Hillsboro, the highway split into a west and east branch, one heading into Forth Worth, the other delving deep into the heart of Dallas. On those roads I spotted the signs for Italy and Ennis, the nightmares from the other night threatening to overwhelm my thoughts. It was my hometown, and I still had family living there—distant family who tried to convince me to go to church with them and convert any time I saw them. They had never forgiven my father for marrying a Jew, or for not forcing his kids to convert themselves. But the truth was, my dad had loved us; he wanted us happy, and I think more than that, he loved my mom and wanted her happy. Well, not dying would have done a better job of that—but whatever the reason for him never pressing the issue of religion with mom or us kids, I was grateful for it. Muscle memory tugged at my arms, urging me to take the turnoff towards Ennis. Even after all these years, that dilapidated farmhouse called out to me, begging me to unearth the secrets there. I refused, of course; it was better to let those secrets stay buried and dead.

My mind wandered, unbidden, to Domah—the creature that had trained me in the use of magic and the secret alefbet. I had made promises back then. Of course, things had been set in motion even before my eyes had been opened to the knowledge all around us. Back then, I had felt honored, like I was chosen for a higher purpose; honestly I felt like I was Luke Skywalker being trained to be a Jedi, a secret warrior monk for HaShem. I wish I had understood what was going to happen back then—that I would be asked to lie to the people around me constantly; that I would be forced to choose between living a good life, and living a life where I did good. I might have called Child Protective Services, if that sort of thing could be done to creatures like Domah—but instead, I had been blissfully unaware of the life ahead of me.

As I drove, flipping my headlights on as the sun went down, it occurred to me that Domah had known precisely what was in store for me; he had known every twist and turn that would come my way. I couldn't know that for sure, of course—who could truly understand every capability or the mind of an angelic being? The Beit Din had no way of attaining that sort of clairvoyance; in fact, that sort of magic was strictly prohibited in the Torah. In quick succession in Leviticus, both mediums and oracles are strictly forbidden. "Being around them makes you unclean;" "Being around them cuts you off from the Jewish people;" and of course, the old standby, "Any man or woman who is involved in the practices of mediums or oracles shall be put to death. They shall be pelted to death with stones." People in the old times sure loved their rocks.

The rabbis of my synagogue maintained that this was not supposed to be read literally, but rather, figuratively—that the ancient law-keepers and rabbis would bend over backwards to avoid a death sentence. Maybe that's true, but in most cases, I think when someone is an actual necromancer it's probably safest to be done with them for good. Mediums were probably fine; besides, I wasn't a fundamentalist, and I had a hard time believing a loving god penned any sentence that involved killing people. I think it's far more likely that there were enemy tribes who made use of those practices, and this was merely ancient propaganda against those tribes. Of course, I still stayed away from those practices, as did most of my colleagues—but even without knowing the exact details of what my life would entail, the Beit Din knew enough. They knew I would be in life-threatening situations and would have to go head-to-head against things that would test not only my endurance, but my sanity, as well. I noticed my hands were gripping the steering wheel harder than necessary. Maybe I had more anger towards my employers than I realized. But what option did I have? I had no resume at all, and my only possible lucrative skills would get me a job in academia, which certainly wasn't the place for me.

Of course, I was being dramatic because I was in the middle of a hard case. Most of my work didn't involve fighting off cults or being stabbed in my own house. Most days I spent in meditation or studying lore over Ethiopian food on Congress. That had been Rivkah's doing; when I first began training her— which mostly meant her picking at my brain—she had insisted on going to a different restaurant representing the diaspora every day. I assume she had that rule because I was paying at the time; she certainly stopped wanting to go out as often once I had stopped expensing all of her food. When I did have a case, it was usually a simple exorcism, sometimes redirecting some sort of cryptid. The worst—on a typical day—would be negotiating with an angry Sheydim that felt it had been slighted in some way.

There were cases like this—things that had me going up against groups of people or monsters that were stronger and more dangerous than I was. My body and psyche bore the scars of claws and tendrils and hate that had been borne from outside the world I knew. I had gone into the proverbial wild, and had come back from the cold—more often than not—a changed man. How many more trips into the wilderness before I ceased being Ze'ev? Would I be a wild creature, fit to be put down—or at that point, would I have become the scapegoat that was given to atone for the sins of the Beit Din?

Dallas was always a pain in the ass to drive through; heavy traffic, and people who drove like they didn't care who lived or died. It was distracting enough to pull me away from my melancholy thoughts and focus my mind on the task at hand. I reached over and thumbed at my phone until I found music that was a bit more energetic; something to help me pump up for what was about to go down. Unlike Austin, Dallas had bad areas—places where leaving even my shitty car alone would be a bad idea. Of course, the warehouse—Basken's warehouse—was close to such an area. I parked the car and watched the building for a few minutes,

I wondered if Basken lived close; I doubted it—

something told me that this man was careful. He had minions throughout the South, and had set traps for me in a few places now. He likely rented this place and lived somewhere else entirely to avoid detection. If I was lucky, he would be close to Austin; if I was unlucky, he would be in another state entirely. If I had managed to get the dybbuk's name in Memphis, I could have looked up where he was buried and really narrowed down my search—but such is life. Outside the front of the nondescript warehouse were signs stating that it was for lease; clever, careful man. Except slowly it dawned on me that the man I had interrogated in my dreams earlier could have been lying, saying anything to keep safe a few more moments. Occam's Razor would state that this had been a wild goose chase, and that I was, in fact, an idiot. I could find him again so long as we had his little totems, but the idea that I had wasted half a day driving to Dallas rankled something fierce. There was only one thing to do; I parked a few streets over—as close to a nicer neighborhood as I could—and sat in my car for a few moments, taking the time to slip into a meditative state. The couple of minutes that it took to force myself to be more aware and sensitive to what was happening at the moment was a minimal price to pay. Once I was satisfied, I stepped out of the car and made my way towards the warehouse.

One thing that separates me from most people who use the title of "operative" is that I don't generally deal with human opponents all that often. While I had served some time in the Israeli army, even that had been a deployment of unusual circumstance. I hadn't been on the front lines, so to speak; essentially, I had been a counter-guerrilla fighter. But one thing I did know was how to clear a building.

I did my best to approach the warehouse stealthily, looking for alternative entrances to the front doors. After a few moments of searching, I found a side door with a simple padlock on it—and me without any tools with which to pick a lock; just my luck. Fortunately, a couple more minutes of searching yielded a nearby window that was hanging slightly open; otherwise, I would have had to go in the front door.

I slipped in through my lucky window; with my right hand I swung my knife open, flipping it easily into a reverse grip. I didn't plan on letting anyone get the drop on me this time. The warehouse was mostly quiet, but I could hear murmuring coming from deeper within. I continued to creep, watching over my shoulder for any sign of someone trying to get the drop on me. It was a normal warehouse, essentially a big empty room divided into hallways. This particular warehouse was attempting to look mostly abandoned. A thick coat of dust lay on most of the boxes here, but that was just lazy housekeeping; the floor was littered with footprints in the dust—and drag-marks, like someone had been dragged between two people. Despite the sounds of talking that I could hear from further inside the warehouse, everything else was silent. There was something wrong here.

Within my focused awareness, I made a checklist of every sensation I was feeling: I could hear murmuring, and my footfalls, as soft as they were, resounded in my ears like I was shaking the earth; my breath was slow and steady, each one measured and taken intentionally. The knife in my hand was cool to my touch, and the hand itself was loose and ready to move like a snake striking if it needed to. My eyes had adjusted to the darkness, and I had no trouble navigating around the warehouse. So what was wrong? As soon as you become hyper-aware of something not happening, you drop out of meditation; you are no longer in the moment—worse still, you never notice it when it happens.

I continued to sneak my way through the building, only to stop outside the door of some kind of office. I could hear voices on the other side; they were muffled and I couldn't make out what they were saying. I only counted two different voices, although that was hardly reassuring—two voices meant at least two people; there could always be more. I opened the door as quietly as I could and darted into the room, knife at the ready. I was late to the party; the place had been staged just for my arrival—a single folding-chair with a tablet in a little easel faced the body of a young woman, who was sprawled on the floor, unmoving; the voices were coming from the tablet. I had once again been played, by someone who always seemed to be three or four steps ahead—even after all the trouble I went through with the dream walking.

I moved to the body to check for a pulse, but I knew it was too late. From the bruising on her throat, it looked like she had been strangled; but judging from the blood on the floor, she had been stabbed at least a few times. I glanced up at the tablet; I already knew what I would see, and sure enough, it was in the middle of a video call, and standing in view of the camera was a man in a black robe and a crimson mask. Other than the crimson colors and gold filligree, it looked like one of those plague-doctor masks; I assumed this was Basken.

"My followers are loyal to me, exorcist. My minions come when I call, fight when I command it, and die when it serves me best—not always in that order, of course." I jumped back at the taunt, sure that the woman before me would rise from her position to attack me, just like Yash from the morgue had done before. From the tablet—probably in another city—Basken laughed. "No, no; don't worry, she is serving a different purpose."

"You are a sick sack of shit, Basken." It was always best practices to belittle and mock people like this; someone who had given themselves so many titles would definitely have an inflated ego. "Your reaction to me hitting the two deluded morons that follow you has been to murder two people."

"Their lives were mine to end, and their deaths served me."

"Not well enough; Yash is still in the morgue, and I'm not."

The necromancer's head tilted; was that a sign of frustration—or was he merely acknowledging that so far, all of his tricks and traps had failed? Hell, his best trap so far had been just existing, while putting me on a collision course with ghouls.

"Yes . . . how did you manage to destroy my minion??" he finally asked. That was good—he didn't know about my traditions; he had blind spots.

"That's for me to know and for you to find out

when I ram my fist down your throat and throw you to the cops."

"To the police?" Basken laughed from behind the stupid crimson mask. "I would be interested to know how they arrest people on charges of dark magic!"

"You are an idiot—tampering with corpses, murder, conspiracy to commit murder, grave desecration; those are also real laws, which you broke in the pursuit of power." That actually made Basken pause; that was a problem for a lot of true practitioners—they saw everything as a nail for their particular hammer. They forgot the other details of what was happening in the world.

"Yes, murder . . . murder would be a serious crime—like how Marcus is now being charged with Yash's murder; he had time to warn me about you, but was still caught in your trap, so I thought, well, now—isn't turnabout fair play?"

I realized too late what he was implying; I had been so focused on the psychopath on the tablet that I hadn't been listening to anything else. Outside the moment, I had utterly missed the sound of approaching sirens—and me here, with the corpse of a murdered woman.

I had to think fast; I pocketed my knife and used the sleeve of my jacket to grab at the tablet, which fell onto the floor and landed partially in the congealed blood of Basken's victim. I spat a curse; I could still hear Basken laughing at his brilliant plan. I had to admit that it was good; I wasn't exactly sure how I would get out of this one. I scooped up the tablet, still using my sleeves to handle the device before moving as quickly as I could toward the exit.

CHAPTER IX

OUTSIDE, I COULD see the flashing lights of incoming police and emergency vehicles. There was a voice in my head that said that waiting for the police and explaining that the victim was dead when I arrived would be the smart decision; but then I would need to explain why I had come to Dallas, broken into a warehouse, and taken evidence—all without mentioning the zombie cult. I was also probably a person of interest in that case back in Austin, with the dead-again undead-again cultist whose corpse I had mutilated. Maybe waiting for the police wasn't the best decision before me. The tablet went in my coat pocket; I wanted to handle it as little as possible—it would be shitty to have my fingerprints on something connected to a murder. As I ran through the alleyways of this shitty warehouse district, I realized that I probably should have just left the damn thing back there. Now I had taken the best possible tool for stopping Basken away from them by not thinking straight. I could see the blue and red strobes of patrol cars getting closer; who knew what he had told them to set them on my trail? Would they even stop to ask questions, or would I be cut down down in the street by trigger-happy gunmen?

I would be damned if my little war with this upstart necromancer would end with me going to prison. I doubted I would survive long in a place populated by the Aryan Brotherhood. I assessed my options for a moment: I could try to tap into some magic, use a mashiva[50] to bring forth angelic might to assist me—but that seemed a bit much, and the silent aleph was a nuclear option that was as dangerous to me as it was to anyone else. I doubted the amulet I wore with my dog tags could protect me from being noticed by a full police force specifically searching for me. That left me running for my damn life with a butterfly knife.

As I fled down another street, I kept watch over my shoulder; when your whole life was dealing with ghosts and scary shit, you often forget about the genuine danger of entirely human threats. Now I was acutely aware of them—as a lone Jewish white boy running through the projects of Dallas, I stood out like a sore thumb. Of course, it did play into my favor; the police were less likely to be enthusiastic about following me into this neighborhood, and the people living here were less likely to work with cops. None of that helped me much if someone decided I was an easy target, however.

While I was jogging through a nearby alleyway, it became clear how genuinely terrible my situation was; I was fleeing from the police after being set up for murder—possibly for the second time—and in Dallas. I had forgotten that the dark and cramped paths and my injuries would make me easy hunting for another group I had managed to piss off. My first

---

50 A miracle

and only warning came as I stumbled, and the too-many-jointed, claw-tipped hand of a ghoul ripped through the air where my head would have been. I growled in frustration as I continued my flight; I wasn't as fast as a ghoul, and now I needed to hide my presence as much as they did.

"This isn't a good time!" I shouted over my shoulder at the ghoul that emerged from the house; it didn't answer me, not that I had expected it to. Unlike most ghouls—but very much in keeping with Baalrachius—this ghoul was sporting a specially tailored suit instead of rags. I was reminded of Slenderman, the creepypasta—and I had to wonder if this ghoul was responsible for those legends. Most ghouls were more feral than cognizant, acting on impulse and instinct rather than strategy. Instead of the usual snarling visage of a vicious animal this ghoul looked calm; determined. It was just my luck that Baalrachius would decide to send something as terrible as this ghoulish hitman after me.

I couldn't outrun the creature, and I wasn't as strong. Usually, I could use some limited sorcery, or outwit ghouls—but I wasn't sure that would work this time. Add to this that I had already been running, while my pursuer was fresh to the chase; things were not looking great for me. I slipped my knife from my pocket; it seemed I was going to rack up another ghoul kill. At this rate, I was actually going to justify their hunting of me. I spun on my heel, suddenly changing direction and taking two steps forward to attempt to bring my knife into the ghoul's solar plexus.

He was faster than me, his reflexes more honed;

his hand blocked my arm, and his other palm slammed into my chest, knocking me back and away—for a moment I had trouble catching my breath, but it didn't feel like any of my ribs had been broken. I gasped, and stood as straight as the pain would allow me. Now that I wasn't attacking or running, the ghoul stood watching me, waiting, alert for what my next move would be. It seemed odd that his attack had only pushed me back, and that the ghoul hadn't used its claws to tear out my stomach. Slowly, I showed both of my hands and flipped the knife closed. If I was wrong, I would die in a moment.

"You aren't here to kill me?" I asked. The creature stood; now that I had the time to really look at it, I could see that stretched out, he was probably close to eight feet tall. He shook his head before reaching into his pocket and pulling out a long, foul-smelling cigarette, and lit it. He took a few puffs of his cigarette, the cherry glowing an evil-looking green; I imagined that I wouldn't be able to find his brand on store shelves—at least not anywhere humans shopped.

"Don't get it twisted, human; there is a bounty on your head—one that would propel me further into power and status in the courts of the monstrous, should I collect it." I didn't know ghouls had courts, or any society beyond what I had seen from Baalrachius. "But you see, I am not newly grown; I have acted as assassin and executioner long enough to grow tired of it." Somewhere out there, the police were growing closer, but I was undoubtedly outmatched at the moment, so I stayed still and nodded. "I know why the price on your head is in place, and I know you are not the one who is fucking with my food supply." He inhaled deeply, and his eyes focused on my pocket.

"You're a native to Dallas, then; funny that Shalnacht has never mentioned you before."

"You think that lowly insect fears you more than I?" he shook his head and flicked his cigarette at me. I didn't flinch, letting it hit me in the chest and then fall to the ground. Even if the ghoul wasn't planning on killing me, I didn't trust it enough to take my eyes off of it, for even a moment. "If you die, then that trash necromancer will continue to work, and it could lead my people to act impulsively, which in turn could lead to a war between your kind and mine." I had to assume it meant hunters and people in the know, rather than specifically Jews. I nodded again, this time understanding a bit more.

"Why tell me any of this? Why not just kill the necromancer yourself? I mean, you had no problem finding me; just go to his house while he's asleep, and have at him," I suggested.

"I had your scent from your little scuffle; we all have your scent, little Wolf." I hated that they kept calling me that. My name, Ze'ev, was Hebrew for wolf, and sometimes I had gone by Wolf to my simpler friends back home. Hearing it coming from things like Baalrachius and this creature was like hearing a predatory middle-aged man call a child "honey." "So, you can find the necromancer and deal with it."

"Okay," I nodded, hoping I could pretend that he hadn't just dropped a bombshell of supernatural terror on me. "So we work together, find the necromancer, and then I hand him over to you; that way, you get your . . . " The figure raised its hand, bringing me up short.

"No; I'm simply not going to kill you, or tell my brothers and sisters where to find you—everything else you can do on your own." Something clicked, the beginning of a plan forming slowly in my mind. I nodded; that was likely the best I was going to get from this creature.

"Do you have a name?"

"You can call me Mr. Grin; it is not my name, but it will suffice for now."

"And you could have picked a less creepy name; okay, Mr. Grin, hope to not see you again." I darted past him, my only goal now to loop around back towards my vehicle and make a clean escape back to Austin.

I made it through the rest of the dicey area without any more molestation. I don't know how much of that had been Mr. Grin's doing and how much was blind luck, but either way, I offered my thanks to HaShem. I used my phone to call a rideshare service; it would be the easiest way to get back to my car and get into my vehicle. Within a few moments, a young man in a beat-up Subaru drove up and opened a door for me. It was a long way from the nicer rides I got when leaving an airport, but it would do for now. I slipped in the back seat and let the sludgy hip-hop coming from the speakers wash over me.

"How you doing tonight, man?" the driver asked. I cracked open an eye, watching him; he seemed to spend as much time looking at me through the rearview mirror as he spent looking at the road—maybe this hadn't been the safest choice.

"I'm fine. I just need to get back to my car."

"Cool, cool; so, you're Jewish?" Why was it these drivers could never get the hint when someone just wanted a ride, not a conversation? I assumed he asked due to the kippah that was still somehow on my head.

"Yeah. I am."

"Yeah, we pray for y'all, all the time; you know we have a lot of love for Jews, like we support Israel and everything, you know, y'all are God's chosen people." This was nothing new, though when I had lived in New York or Israel, no one had ever felt it necessary to approach me and tell me how important my people were to them. It felt hollow, like every prayer was really a prayer that we would accept their way of doing things, and stop stubbornly clinging to our old ways. I had studied Christian theology, and its apocalypse was particularly unkind to Jews. The long history of persecution, blood libel, and pogroms hardly helped. This man was probably ignorant of all of that; he was merely doing what his parents told him to, without any of the conscious hate or malice. His simply had the privilege of belonging to the largest religious group in the country. I gave him a tight-lipped smile and nodded, hoping that would be enough.

"What brings you to this area, man? Do Jews smoke weed?" There was just enough of a pause in his question to make me feel like he was uncomfortable asking. I stared at him hard; it was quite a leap. "I mean no offense, but this neighborhood sort of has a reputation; I mean I'm not judging, everyone needs to do their own thing." I considered ignoring him or reprimanding him—certainly not giving him a good rating—but then I thought about it; it was as good an alibi as any.

"Yes, some Jews smoke pot, to calm nerves, or manage pain; it has a lot of good uses—besides, HaShem, er, G-d, made everything, including marijuana . . . so how can we condemn it as bad or evil?" It was an argument I heard from weed activists every time I ventured outside in Austin. In truth, I agreed; for the most part, a plant that could manage pain and symptoms so easily seemed to have been placed here by HaShem to aid us. It just seemed to be a fight that no one would win, when forced to go against the real evil of big pharmaceutical corporations. The young man nodded; surely these were thoughts he had heard, and likely voiced himself in the past.

"Don't worry brother; I wouldn't turn someone in just for enjoying some pot, but if the cops pulled us over for some reason, you're on your own—I can't afford to deal with that." I nodded; smart kid, and friendly enough. I let my eyes close again. Hopefully he thought I was just high, rather than ignoring him.

"I'm not holding, but all the same, maybe you should drive carefully—to avoid having to deal with police at all." He took my advice to heart, and must have decided to let me enjoy my high as I rested in his back seat. It would be a short ride; I had only run a couple of miles—if that—but I needed to get some rest before I tried to make it back to Austin, and then I had to decide what to do next. How did I go from the mouse to the cat in this game?

When I got back to my car, all I had to do was drive home at an even pace and not get pulled over. Inside my pocket was the tablet that Basken had left at the murder scene. While I was relieved that I hadn't been caught in his snare, I was furious I hadn't stopped him there—and another person was dead, and unlike the would-be-killer Yash, this one was entirely my fault. I had to stop Basken.

Driving out of Dallas, I wished I owned a police scanner, it just wasn't something I had ever needed before. While I had faced people before, and I had faced intelligent monsters before, I had never been in a situation where I needed to go head-to-head with law enforcement. Not knowing what was happening, what sort of details Basken had given the cops, was painful. I also still didn't know how much Basken even knew about me.

I took a moment to review what Basken definitely knew; he knew I was an exorcist, and where I lived. If he had discovered all of that by scrying, he would also know I was Jewish; other than that, I should be safe— I had started carrying my obscuring amulet after that first attack. The fact that no one had attacked or even harassed Sara, Rivkah or my mother had to mean that Basken didn't know any more than what he had already used against me.

I had been driving for just under an hour when I realized I was being followed. They hadn't popped their sirens yet, but I recognized the sheriff's car behind me in the distance. My blood ran cold when I saw the unlit lights above the car; this was just as bad as any possible scenario. If I ended up caught now, with the tablet in my pocket and any prints they found at the ME's office in Austin, I would be unable to convince anyone of my innocence—especially when combined with the weapon in my pocket, and the gun in my dash. I would be forced to try and explain way too much, and would more than likely end up in an asylum without any help from anyone, least of all the Beit Din. They weren't big on interference; hell, I might get sacked when this was all over, even if I didn't get arrested.

But until he flipped on that siren, there was still hope. I glanced around to see what exit I was closest to when my stomach dropped again. Exit 386, Ennis; it looked like I was going back home, whether I wanted to or not. I had to wonder if this wasn't pure serendipity; if there were forces at work that had manipulated events to create the necessity. It looked like my nightmares were going to get a chance to come true. If they wanted me to relive the worst day of my life, I might as well get this over with. I turned off the highway and started speeding towards Ennis; so did my new sheriff friend.

I pressed down on the gas, just enough to pull ahead but without enough speed to make the sheriff take notice that I was now actively trying to put distance between us. My plan at this point depending on him or her thinking I was still ignorant of their pursuit. When I felt there was enough of a gap between us, I pulled off onto the main road, quickly maneuvering my car through several turns to get me into a driveway between a diner and thrift shop before killing the engine and turning off every light. I held my breath, waiting, and praying; and after a few moments, I saw the Sheriff pass in the rearview mirror, speeding down the road, trying to discover to where I had disappeared.

CHAPTER X

AS SOON AS I was sure the Sheriff had finished patrolling the main street searching for me, I left my hidey-hole; no doubt he would be letting the local law enforcement know I was here, and all it would take is one overzealous country bumpkin with a badge to ruin everything. Of course, I was also assuming a lot—that was the worst part of being ignorant; that sheriff might just want to pull me over for expired plates or speeding. It could be nothing—or it could be that he thought I was a serial killer, working my way across Texas, and was following my car because it matched a description that Basken had given to the police in Dallas. I knew where I was being led. I hit the road and began driving as fast as I could without arousing suspicion—towards Crisp; towards my childhood home. My body knew the route, as much as I wished it would just forget everything about these roads. Within a few minutes, I had found my way through those North Texas backroads on which I had learned to drive, and into Crisp; of course, I wouldn't just walk into the barn tonight. I maneuvered my car through the opening left by the broken double doors, and once again shut everything off. I felt like I got out of the area pretty easily—but I couldn't be positive that no one had ID'd me.

At one point, Crisp had been a small Texas town, but in 1954 something happened, and the population fell below a hundred. They shut down the post office, and within the decade the entire town was nothing more than a few scraggly houses and ranches, with a general store near the main intersection. Of course, even that had closed down, in favor of my uncle's shop in Bristol. Now the population hovered around the mid-twenties, and even that was a few stubborn older folks and their kids, who felt terrible about leaving their parents. I don't know what happened in the fifties; even my great uncles and grandfather couldn't tell me what had driven away the entire population of the small town. I had my suspicions; I believed it all came back to what had happened just outside of this barn.

I must have stayed seated in the car for a good ten minutes, staring out at the dark surroundings in silence. I might tell someone it was to make sure I wasn't followed, but the truth of the matter was, despite my bravado in coming here, I was terrified. Everything was as it had been in my dreams, minus the corpses of friends. The beams holding the building up were rotted near to death, and worm-eaten debris sat all around. In one corner, a few bones were all that was left of the cow's body from so long ago. Everything was the same as it had been twenty years ago. The silence—then and now—was crushing. It took me a few moments to realize that I couldn't hear the sounds of locusts or birds—no distant hum of cars on the highway, or trains roaring by on old tracks. Everything was still and silent.

There had been three times in my life where I had experienced such extreme silence; each time I had been here, and it solidified the idea that coming here had not been my decision, and that the police and ghouls pursuing me had all just been tools to lead me here under his guidance. I put my head on the steering wheel; I didn't have the time for this right now, for games played under the guise of mentorship or help. I needed to figure out a way to stop Basken, not chase my own tail with inhuman creatures. I heard a knock on the window, but I didn't look up; my irritation—bordering on rage—was subsuming my fear. I was tired of being a pawn, and didn't feel up to pretending awe. There was another knock on the window; without looking, I unlocked the door and pulled myself out, keeping my eyes straight ahead. After several moments of staring into the darkness of the barn, I felt his hand on my shoulder.

Despite my irritation, exhaustion, and stress, I felt relief flood through my body at his touch. Even that irritated me, and slowly, even that irritation melted away. I stepped away from his hand; it was a nearly painful disconnect, but for me to converse without bias, I needed to be able to feel. I walked a few steps away, watching the stars through the broken doors. I always forgot how filled the night sky was when I was in the cities. It was beautiful; space was filled with the empty spaces I feared with my whole being, but down here, it didn't appear empty at all. Out here, the number of stars was mind-boggling and beautiful. Finally, I glanced over. He looked—well, he looked the same as he always did; beautiful, with perfect skin and a kind face. I realized with a start that he resembled a kinder, browner Clint Eastwood, from *The Good the Bad and the Ugly*; funny how I had never noticed that before—but then again, I had never been a huge fan of Westerns. Of course, this wasn't his real face; it was the face and mannerisms that were pulled from the minds of the populace—a facade that would shift and change as he shifted and moved. His features were smoothly altering, to portray what would best match with comfort and safety. I suppose I should be happy that he didn't look like a TV preacher or shitty politician, with the local population influencing him.

"You seem on edge." Domah didn't speak. I don't mean in this particular instance; I mean that throughout my entire life, through everything that I had experienced beside the creature now standing before me, he had never spoken. It took me a moment to realize that even now, he wasn't speaking. There, sitting on Domah's shoulder, was a field mouse. Domah had communicated in the past through visions, exaggerated hand signs, and sometimes through writing in the dirt with his finger; never through speech. And that was how it should be; Domah was the angel of silence.

Domah was also the figure from my nightmares—the distressed, perfectly beautiful man, standing opposite the doorway from the creature that stalked my fears. Now, he seemed somehow less real than he did in my dreams; this at least was something I was used to, the ephemeral nature of my mentor. I watched him for a few moments, anger warring with concern and, well, adoration. Despite my attempts to stay angry, Domah was an angelic being, and everything about him screamed holiness. A true piece of divinity that validated everything I believed and everything that I practiced.

"Yes," I finally managed to say. "I am on edge; I don't suppose you've been keeping up, but things have been a bit on the shitty side, lately." He cocked his head at me. I wasn't sure if that meant he hadn't been aware—which seemed impossible—or if it just meant I should unburden myself. "I'm fighting a cult, they're necromancers; so, that's sort of what I'm in the middle of right now." He nodded, and then the field mouse opened its mouth and what I could only assume is Domah's voice spoke out from its tiny lips.

"I see; all in the course of your duties to your people, I assume." It was odd, listening to his voice; I had assumed he had no voice at all until now, but he also inflected like someone who had never spoken before—each word was a simple and utterly monotone statement. He stepped back further into the shadows, and I realized that he was listening for something; perhaps he was immune to the crushing silence surrounding him. "And the local guardsmen are hunting you, I believe; did you know you have expired food?" I nodded slightly; his vernacular was off, but that was easy to forgive. "I wanted to speak to you, see to your development." It's probably a sin to laugh in an angel's face, but it isn't ever mentioned in any of the book I've read, so I allowed myself the scoff. When I glanced back, Domah's face seemed as passive as ever, but I could have sworn the mouse wore a confused look.

"Now? You want to guide me now?" I shook my head. "Domah, I am on the run from three separate, disparate groups." I held up a hand and ticked off my fingers. "The cops, a cult, and ghouls. The best thing I can say at the moment is that the cops probably don't want me dead—but even that feels like a stretch. I don't think now is the best time to talk about meditation and seeing white fire on black fire, my friend." I took a few steps back towards my car before turning to face him again; the absurdity of the situation was getting to me. "And what's with the mouse?"

Domah reached up reflexively, protectively I thought, and cupped the mouse in one hand while looking at me with what could only be called worry on a face that had never shown worry before. "This is how I choose to speak. You see this as a problem."

"No; it isn't a problem, Domah. It's just unusual; I think it may not break whatever rules you have, but I think it breaks the spirit of them. You aren't so silent anymore. And something else; why here? Why always here? You don't just exist in this barn, do you? You couldn't just meet somewhere else, like on the San Marcos River, or over off of Lamar in a coffee shop or something, you know, in Austin, where I live? You could come to the office where I actually do all my studying and research, It would be a hell of a lot closer and, I might add, a hell of a lot less traumatic than making me come here again and again."

Domah's eyes hardened a little; I got the distinct feeling that I had overstepped—of course, any reasonable human being would understand how cruel it was to bring me here over and over again, but Domah wasn't human. His mind—if he even had what could be considered a mind—doesn't work the way ours do. I don't think many humans had ever shouted at any angel, let alone Domah. I held up my hand to stop his reprimand, and nodded.

"Fine; you need to be here, bring me here, whatever. But now I don't have time to sit and meditate with you. I need a miracle to get home without getting arrested, not a lesson in Kabbalah."

Domah moved to the edge of the barn peering out, now that I looked too, I could see the flashing lights, the reds and blues heading down the road towards us; even if they didn't know exactly where I was, they knew I was close enough to hunt down. Suddenly Domah turned back and marched to the center of the barn. He kneeled there on his knees directly in front of my car.

"Then a miracle you will have," the mouse said in that ridiculous, deep voice. I turned to face him, about to ask what he was talking about, when there was a sudden crack of thunder shaking the entire barn. The downpour was immediate—rain so hard and fast that it was startling. I peered out of the barn door and reached a hand out, but it was like the rain droplets avoided my flesh. The rain was shaping itself around me. It was a terrifying reminder of the sort of power wielded by the creature towards whom I had just been so glib. I brought my hand back in and turned back towards Domah, stopping short when I discovered he was now directly in front of me. He brought a hand up and put his palm over my eyes. "You know these roads. They are entwined in your DNA. You have no need of sight or headlights for this journey." The voice was no longer coming from the mouse, or from Domah. The words were shaped in the sound of the rain that was slowly permeating the silence of Domah's presence.

When he took his hand away, I was alone in an empty barn; outside, a storm to end all storms raged, thunder crashing overhead. I was sure that it was localized to being just above I-35 heading south. I was also convinced that this was as good of a chance as I would get. I slipped into the driver's seat and hit the gas. In Exodus, one of the final plagues was darkness; various rabbi have argued over how this was done. Of course, the most rational explanation was always the old eclipse of the sun—but I always agreed with the more frightening interpretation; it was suggested that the angel that brought darkness and took the firstborn of the Egyptians was the angel that acted as a barrier, to slow the Egyptians down during their pursuit of the Hebrew people. The darkness itself was the angel Samael—the angel of death—spreading his wings across the sky.

Driving through the rain now, I was reminded of the plague of darkness. I wondered if Domah brought this darkness down, or if he had somehow enlisted the assistance of Samael. The prospect—that above my car, the manifestation of Death was keeping pace with me—was terrifying. I didn't know if angels could invoke angels; I also didn't really understand how angels manifested on earth, like Domah had. I could only hope that the rain was solely Domah's doing.

He was right; I drove down the highway at full

speed, sensing the road rather than seeing it. With my lights off, I should have rocketed off one of the many curves of those North Texas roads, and I found myself often holding my breath, waiting for disaster. The sound of rain was crashing into my car, and that and the constant rumble of my engine were my only companions for this drive; I didn't dare distract myself with music, afraid that if I redirected my kavanah[51] away from the moment, whatever miracle was keeping me from spinning out of control and hidden from the police would be broken.

Those three hours were about the most stressful in my life so far. But at 4 AM, I parked my car in a small parking garage near 6th and Lamar in downtown Austin and closed my eyes. I didn't want to go home, or to Sara—not when there was possibly some heat coming my way; instead I would wait here, get some rest and figure out how to handle things in the morning.

---

51 Intention, and focused willpower.

CHAPTER XI

JHAD SLEPT in worse places, in worse situations. When I was eighteen, I moved from my home in Texas to Israel. I wanted to study there; I was still on the path to becoming a rabbi at that point. I knew that as soon as I moved to Israel, I would be drafted. Service was mandatory for all Israeli citizens, and as a Jew making aliyah[52], I would be considered a citizen. The Beit Dien—already watching me due to my childhood encounter with the dybbuk; I don't think they knew about Domah, or the training he had bestowed on me—didn't stop me; I suspect they may even have greased the wheels. Once I had jumped through all of the hoops and answered every question, I made my way to Michve Alon[53]; luckily, my Hebrew was good enough not to need all that much help, and I was placed into my new unit reasonably quickly. Unit 621, Egoz.

In Egoz, there was no Us vs. Them mentality. I had been prepared for brainwashing—"Behold, the great and holy state of Israel, and our enemies hounding us at every turn that only you can defeat."— but I hadn't received the prerequisite indoctrination.

---

52 Migrating to Israel

53 Basic Training base for the IDF

Instead, after basic, Egoz's drill sergeant—a middle-aged man named Vladimir Tseitlin—drilled us continuously on combat maneuvers. Egoz was a special forces unit that was trained specifically to deal with guerrilla warfare situations. Tseitlin believed that nothing he could teach us would get us ready for dealing with actual warfare, and so, other than a few men and women who simply couldn't make the cut, he essentially rubber-stamped the rest of us onto active duty. It was hellish.

Beyond simply seeing the types of pain and punishment other human beings were enduring, we were easily despised by a vast population. It wasn't just Palestinians; I was pelted with insults from people from all over the world, who had come to Israel specifically to yell at Israeli soldiers. Growing up in America in the era of the Iraq war, I was used to soldiers being treated like heroes. It was pounded through our heads that serving in the military was the single bravest thing anyone could do. There in Israel, walking the dusty, crowded, and angry streets, it was different. Every Israeli has to serve, so we weren't considered brave or extraordinary by the Israelites. We weren't respected by the people we were trying to protect, and seeing the oppressed in Gaza, I had to wonder at the time what we were trying to protect them from.

Even during the terrorist attacks I experienced—fighting house-to-house, face-to-face with people who despised me and wanted me dead because I had been born into a different family, a family of Jews—I could never shake the feeling that all of this was futile. Up until this point in my life, I had really only dealt with a ghost and an angel; I think that Domah shielded me from the other things in Ennis. That would change during my time in the IDF.

I arrived in Israel in February of 2006—which means when Hezbollah launched their attack and abduction of Israeli soldiers in July, I was on hand to be part of the action. Of course, Israel responded to the hostage exchange demands with missiles, and back and forth until it was a full fledged war with missiles, tanks and of course house-to-house fighting. This is the problem with all conflict in that part of the world; the beginning is never visible, and past atrocities excuse current situations which then allow for the next round of atrocities. No matter what I come across in the supernatural world, I have never seen such malevolence as humans who have been taught that another group is their enemy since birth. Humans were the most vindictive of all creatures; personal slights turn into wars that kill thousands. At the end of the day, though, it was soldiers like me who would get nothing out of the conflict, fighting against people who had everything to lose. It was during one of these actions that I had my first encounter with the supernatural as an adult.

"Get down, Avi!" I shouted, as we rounded the corner between two buildings. I had just barely seen the glint off the edge of the rifle's muzzle from a nearby street fire before diving to one side. Bullets tore into the air exactly where I had been not a second before, slamming into the wall—and into Avi. I swore as I crawled on my belly through an open doorway, praying that there wouldn't be any more surprises inside. More gunfire sounded, as the rest of my unit rounded the corner and pushed through the doorway. Irit came through first and lingered in the doorway, providing cover fire for Saul, Uzi, and finally Tobiah, dragging Avi with him as he came through the door. We were in a small two-story house, and Avi was bleeding on the tiles of the kitchen. From where I crouched I could see a dining room, living room, and staircase.

"Where is Mani?" I asked, finally having the wherewithal to stand and move to cover a window, rifle pointed outward, jerking towards any shadow that moved—or that I imagined moving. Uzi shook his head, and Irit spat out a curse; she had always been vocal. "Fuck," I managed to croak out; this was not going according to plan, of course—that was the point of Egoz; we were supposed to be able to roll with the punches, and operate counter to plans backfiring.

"Who are we even fighting?" asked Irit. This got shrugs from the rest of our group.

"Some fucking Arabs; Hezbollah, probably," responded Saul, always ready for the racist angle—although to be fair, it was hard to imagine who else would be attacking us at the moment other than Hezbollah.

"When in question, always blame Hezbollah, right?" Tobiah offered. I shrugged off the banter as I moved to check on Avi; his body armor had caught most of the bullets, but one had gone straight through the meat of his arm, leaving a gushing wound. Pulling bandages from my pack, I began dressing the hole, for the moment just trying to get the bleeding to stop.

"Whoever the fuck it is, we can't stay here; did you get those two outside?" I asked while I patched up Avi, who was just now getting his breath back.

"They aren't shooting at us, are they?" came Irit's retort. I spared a moment to glare at her, and was about to tell her what she could do with her attitude—but at that moment, we heard something from upstairs.

We cut our chatter short, staring up at the ceiling and then glancing to the stairwell. Each step was tortuously slow; flanked by Uzi, Irit, and Tobiah, I gestured that Saul should stay with Avi while we checked it out. Every movement was measured; I was attempting to remain silent and stealthy, while willing my eyes to adjust to the darkness faster. Whoever was up here knew that we were inside; they would have heard the firefight that brought us in. To my ears, my footsteps resounded like the roar of an angry G-d slamming thunder against the Earth—each step screaming out my location to the entire army that was definitely stationed upstairs. I reached the second-floor landing. It looked like any of thousands of rooms. The closed door to the rest of the house was creating a small scene there; debris cluttering the floor, the viscera of families and lives destroyed turning it from home to house and then finally to a warzone. I pushed my imagination down and aside; it wouldn't help me survive.

I kicked open the door, rifle squeezed to my shoulder, sweeping the upstairs rooms from left to right, searching for any sign of an enemy. Irit and Tobiah went past me, clearing a couple of rooms up there, before coming back with a shrug of their shoulders. For a few seconds, we assumed that whatever we had heard before was gone. We were proved wrong when a sudden scream shattered the approximation of silence we had been attempting. The sound didn't echo around us; it came from downstairs, and was cut off as suddenly as it had come.

All four of us rushed downstairs, all thoughts of stealth or tactics gone in that moment of mind-shattering terror. I exploded into the downstairs living room and swung my gun light around. Where we had left Avi and Saul was now the site of atrocity. Saul had been torn apart, his lower jaw missing entirely; his remains had been strewn about. While staring into his lifeless, horror-filled eyes, I wondered where the rest of his chest and body were. A sucking gasp made me spin the light over to Avi.

Avi's mouth worked open and shut, trying to scream but unable to pull any hint of breath from his lungs. In the peripheral of the light, I could see the movement of something hunched over him. I didn't want to move the beam of light; as horrifying as Avi's pale panicked face was, I didn't want to see what loomed over him. It reminded me too much of that thing from the barn; it threatened to bring the nightmares back. I didn't want to know what was making that wet, chewing noise. The choice of avoidance was stolen from me when, seconds after I descended the stairs, the beams from Irit's Uzi's and Tobiah's flashlights landed on the shape that was bent over Avi. It looked like a large person wearing a ragged cloak that hid their face. It was squatting over our teammate; the smell of offal and blood permeated the room, coming off of the thing in waves. Blood coated the front of the figure's robe, and the hood bobbed slightly with every chewing noise it made.

As we watched, a gnarled hand descended, pushing into Avi's stomach, and came back up clutching gobs of meat. The hand was a pallid white, like the underbelly of some scarred and cancerous fish. The long, gnarled fingers each ended in curved talons that glinted dully like iron in the beams of light. It moved in small jerks as it brought the meat and gore to its hood and resumed the chewing noises. We were so horrified that it took us a few seconds to react to what we saw. Our minds were reeling at what was happening—some sort of cannibal had overwhelmed an armed special forces soldier, and was eating our friend. Irit reacted first.

Irit reacted first. "The fuck . . . " she snarled, a growl forming deep in her throat even as she brought her rifle up. Bullets tore through the floor and wall, and each of us followed suit, opening fire on the cannibal. I didn't know if the others saw the friendly fire that killed Avi; I didn't know if it was an accident, or if it had been done to put him out of his pain and horror. I tore my eyes from my dying friend's face in time to see the robed figure half-turn and dart away. Its skin was so white that it almost seemed luminous, but there was nothing beautiful there. Corruption covered its body; sores wept pus, and scars that had healed and then been pulled back open were everywhere. Its face was horribly normal; old and feminine, like any old Bubbie but for the paleness of the flesh and the bright blood that coated her chin and teeth. Its eyes were glowing, illuminating that distressingly-human face with a hateful golden glow. When she moved, she was a dancer, tattered rotting robes swirling about her spinning form. Graceful in a way I had never seen before, she seemed to land for only a heartbeat before leaping again. We followed her with our guns, but couldn't catch her.

I had the distinct feeling she was playing with us, dodging our bullets and letting us run ourselves dry. The four of us—special forces trained soldiers wielding automatic rifles—were no match for this woman in rags. I dropped my rifle, letting it hang from the strap while I dug for something in my backpack, looking for anything that could give us an edge. It was while I was distracted that the woman— if it was a woman—launched her counterattack. I had been looking down, tearing through my pack, when I felt the bullet hit my vest and knock me off my feet. Looking up, it was apparent what had happened; she had spun and danced into our line, and Tobiah, suffering from tunnel vision, had followed her with his rifle. I had been lucky; the bullets that hit me had hit the vest. Uzi, a full head shorter than me, had been less fortunate. I watched the light go out of his eyes, while I screamed at Tobiah to stop shooting. I could have saved my breath; gracefully as though extending a tender caress, the taloned hand of the cannibal woman tore out Tobiah's throat with a single swipe. I remember the ruby droplets of blood spraying through the air, nearly sparkling as they hit the beams of light. My hand closed on what I was looking for, and I looked up to find the woman again. It was only then that I realized all of the gunfire and sound had stopped. The near-silence was filled only with the gurgling gasps of Tobiah dying and the sickening chewing sounds. It took me a moment to locate them again, and when I did, it was difficult not to retch. The cannibal woman had thrown Irit through a wall, and used one of the broken pipes to impale her through the back of the skull. The jagged end of the pipe jutted from her eye socket, a look of rage and horror written across her now-dead face.

At the time, I had nearly given up; what could I do against such a demon? This creature had killed every one of my friends, and we had done nothing to provoke it. I glanced down, realizing my fingers maintained a white-knuckled grip on the item for which I had been searching; I didn't think it would work, but I owed it to my squad to try to save their bodies from being devoured. I owed it to my family to survive. I pulled the pin and waited, counting in my mind, praying I wouldn't mess it up. Waiting until the last possible moment, I lobbed the object at the cannibal. She heard me—or some supernatural sense allowed her to sense the attack—and she turned, opening a cruel mouth so wide that it seemed like she would swallow the world into that dark, needle-lined hole. Before it reached her, the concussion grenade went off.

I had been ready for the bright flash and the wave of force; as soon as it was safe to do so, I jumped up from behind Uzi's body—which I had used as a shield from the blast—and began firing. The creature was no longer dancing. Now she was roaring, swinging her claws wide, hoping to catch me by pure luck. I pumped round after round into the thing until finally, as my clip nearly ran dry, she fell and struck the floor.

To my horror, the ragged cloak continued to writhe on the ground, and hundreds of snakes and insects began to emerge from underneath.

"You can't protect anybody." The voice was a whispered knife, dragged through mud, blood and slime. I turned towards it just in time to see Irit—with a hole straight through her skull—reaching for me with a sneer.

CHAPTER XII

WOKE UP covered in sweat again, my heart beating
so hard that I thought I might vomit it up to ease
the tension in my chest. Nightmare. I seemed to be
having a lot of nightmares lately. This one was mostly
true to history, though Irit hadn't risen from the dead
at any point, to my knowledge. A few years later, after
training with the Beit Din, I had returned to Israel and
hunted down the alukah[54]. It had been a hard battle
then, too, though no one had died other than the
creature. I had removed her head and stuffed her
mouth with dirt myself, before burying her in cement.
I wondered at the time if she remembered me. Not
that it mattered; now she was gone, and dreaming
about that night would do me no favors. I sat up and
adjusted the car seat to rise with me. My back felt like
shit, but that was just the price of sleeping in a car. I
took a moment to wake up, letting my fear response
die down from the nightmare while I checked my
phone. There was a text message from an unknown
number, with an attached image.

It simply read 'YOU CAN'T PROTECT
ANYBODY.' The picture looked like something
snapped from a prison security camera, grainy and ill-

54 Horse-leech, it is often used to refer to a vampiric monster.

defined—but I recognized the person in the picture. It was that cultist on whom I had gotten the jump while dreamwalking.

Marcus, if Basken could be believed. It looked like he was hanging from a sheet in a prison cell. I tossed the phone into the passenger seat, scowling at it. It was one thing to send people to kill me, but invading my dreams felt like a violation. I needed to get a jump on what was happening; I needed to get one step ahead of Basken, instead of being one step behind. If that Marcus was actually dead, I needed to find out more—like how much he had actually told the police. Was I a wanted man, despite Domah's best efforts? Luckily, I wasn't completely friendless.

I grabbed the phone, considering tossing it in a nearby dumpster; after all, it was obviously compromised. I decided not to; not until Rivkah could save everything useful off of it, anyway. Until I had a chance to replace it, I would have to be a little more careful. I scrolled through my contacts and hit "call." After a few moments, there was a groggy answer.

"Ze'ev? What time is it? Why are you calling at 6 AM?"

"Speak in Hebrew, Alex; I don't think my phone is safe," I said in Hebrew.

"Safe? What are you talking?" Officer Alexander Barman was not as fluent in Hebrew as I would have liked him to be, mostly retaining only what he had learned from Sunday School growing up and the prayers he practiced every Friday night.

"You haven't heard anything about me, have you—no APB, no alerts?"

"APB? What? No. Why would there be?" It was a

fair question, and one I couldn't get into very easily—but knowing I wasn't currently in trouble with the Austin police department went a long way towards making me feel better about my day.

"The important thing, Alex, is I have a piece of evidence for a murder case in Dallas. I can drop it somewhere for an anonymous tip."

"Ze'ev, I no understand. Don't know words." That figured; I was going too fast and getting into vocabulary he would never have needed to know in Hebrew.

"Ok, Alex." I switched back to English. "I have something for you, but you can't let your bosses know how you got it." I heard him groan.

"Illegal?"

"Very, and some of your compatriots in Dallas are going to want to have a look at this."

"Fine; just hold onto it for a few hours, and I'll call you when I'm out working, but you owe me fo . . . " I hung up before he could finish. I needed to get this tablet to the cops; if nothing else, it had a connection to Basken and his cronies—I doubt that everyone had worn gloves every time they messed with the damn thing. That was one minor problem dealt with. Now, I had to figure out how to dodge ghouls and keep everyone safe while a mad necromancer kept killing people for my benefit; time to go back to the lab.

"You are an idiot," Rivkah announced, after I had caught her up on everything that had happened since I left.

"Is that fair?"

"Life isn't fair, but you're an idiot; why would you walk into such an obvious trap?" She was fuming, the silver of her piercings glinting in the dim light of the warehouse as she paced, giving lie to the fact that she was more worried than she was angry.

"You have a better idea?" I asked gently. She rounded on me, jabbing a black-nailed finger into my chest.

"Don't you play that game with me, Zev— answering everything I say with a question; I'm not some clueless blond that isn't wise to your tricks. Questions are not answers."

I grimaced at her; that was probably a blow aimed at Sara. Rivkah had met her a few times, and made no qualms about not being her biggest fan. Rivkah claimed that my girlfriend just gave her the creeps. I answered her jab with a glare.

"Rivkah, I've been doing this long enough to know when I'm walking into a trap; believe it or not, this is not the first time I've gone against some cultists." I didn't mention that it *was* the first time that I had gone against such a powerful cultist, or that the King of Ghouls had decided I needed to die; I doubted either of those tidbits would calm down my erstwhile assistant. She took a deep breath, her shirt straining against her curves as she rubbed her head and then resumed glaring at me. I shrugged and offered her my compromised phone. She looked at it, and then me; disgust was written plain across her face before it broke and she sighed, the concern finally showing through.

"We're friends; right, Zev?" She asked.

"I like to think so."

"Then next time you're walking into a situation that might be dangerous to those around you, could you let me know—as your friend?" She reached out and took the phone from my hand, before turning and walking away. I stood there, hand outstretched for a moment, considering what she had said. The truth was, I had a lot of friends and allies. A lot of people who I used for information or favors. Rivkah, Alex Barman, and Amanda from Ancient Mysteries were just a few. I hadn't thought about it until this moment. Usually, my jobs weren't dangerous to those around me. They were hazardous situations, sure, but they were typically confined. Now I was facing someone with cognitive and strategic abilities; someone who didn't flinch at the idea of hurting or even killing innocent people. I move to my desk and shuffled things around a bit before glancing up.

"I am an idiot."

"Obviously," Rivkah retorted from her workstation, where she was drawing sigils around my phone.

"No; I mean, I've been banging my skull against this problem like it's just something I can beat up." I stood and moved across the space to a large whiteboard, where Rivkah wrote out equations and formulae she was working on. I stared at the emptiness for a moment, before grabbing a dry erase marker and writing 'Basken' at the top of the board. Rivkah watched me; I could see her face moving from anger to mild curiosity as I continued to write all the details I knew about what was going on. When I was finished, I realized I knew very little. I stared at the board, waiting for something to come to me, when from Rivkah's table, my phone started ringing. Scowling at the nearly blank whiteboard, I moved to pick up the phone. On the other end was a high-pitched and strained voice.

"You can't protect anybody." The sound was wrong; its wrongness carried over the phone lines and into my ear, a knife in the mud and muck of Sheol, slithering through my mind to wrap around my throat, like a noose that was slowly tightening. "You couldn't protect me. You couldn't protect that girl; how will you protect yourself?" I realized that it wasn't just fear that was making my throat constrict; invisible hands were squeezing my throat shut, cutting off my air. I threw the phone as far as I could, hoping distance might loosen the stranglehold. It didn't.

I could feel the panic setting in, clouding my judgment—or was that the lack of oxygen getting to my brain? I staggered to the table and rummaged around, looking for anything that could help at this exact moment. Without voice, I couldn't even utter a true letter or word. My ace in the hole was worthless. The edges of my world were closing in, blackness coming to swallow me whole, and in that blackness I could almost hear the laughter of the necromancer. I was dimly aware of Rivkah shouting, I could only hope that whatever was attacking me would not go after her once I was dead. I felt hands, solid hands now, touch my back, and the pressure on my windpipe eased. Rivkah was not panicking; she was shouting words from Torah—psalms, to be specific. The force of faith and the words of Law pulled the entity from my throat, and suddenly I could breathe.

I collapsed on the floor, swallowing huge gulps of air. Every heartbeat brought more color and depth to the world around me, but with my oxygen came explosive pain in the form of a migraine. I looked up and saw the ghostly apparition of Marcus standing above me, a scowl on his face and his eyes burning with hatred. I took over for Rivkah, croaking out each word of the psalm, while I gathered my wits and intention. When I could, I stood and pointed a finger at Marcus. With as much command and volume as my bruised larynx could manage, I banished him— hopefully, to a better place. When he was gone, I collapsed again; Rivkah started forward, but I waved her away.

"Burn the phone," I rasped. Thankfully, she didn't question my order, but hurried to fulfill it. Exorcisms were tricky things; they didn't always take, and with the state I was in, I didn't want any surprises from Marcus making a return appearance. I glanced back at the whiteboard and chewed on my lip; perhaps I wasn't as many steps behind as I thought. The initial attack in my home was probably meant to make sure there were no loose ends. Basken was spending more and more energy, tampering with greater and greater power every time he came after me. Not only that; eventually he would catch the attention of other exorcists or operatives. He was sticking his neck out, and I was going to take advantage of that—but instead of going in blind and swinging again, I wanted to make sure I was as many steps ahead as possible. I picked up the dry erase marker and started writing again.

He had now killed and resurrected two of his own

cultists; maybe three, depending on who the woman in the warehouse was. He could scry, summon ghosts and bring corpses to life as zombies—that meant he was no slouch. He would have other tricks up his sleeve. But he was also a necromancer; that meant that his spellwork would be almost entirely focused on death and manipulating the dead. I set down my marker and moved to the corner of the warehouse where I kept our library.

There are countless books on magic and mysticism throughout the world, most written to make a quick buck without any true belief behind the pages. Some were written to try to build up status and power, with real belief but no practical working. Some were written with incredibly powerful workings inside, that are only accessible to a very specific few who have taken the time to master them. The Sefer Yetzirah, or book of creation, is one such book. Readily available in book stores, the secrets inside are very easy to find—but very few have been able to unlock how those secrets might be used. One such person was Rabbi Jochan Samuelsson, my tutor from the Beit Din. I smiled as I leafed through the worn pages of my copy of the text and moved back to the whiteboard.

"Rivkah, we're going to need to prepare and to make a few things before I set out." I picked up the marker to begin designing my defense.

It took a few hours to get everything together. Rivkah's perfectionist nature, so at odds with her aesthetic, forced us to move slower than I would have ideally wanted—but on the other hand, her intense concentration and kavanah at every turn were what made her so good at what she did. So, I sat patiently while she worked. Truth be told, I relished the opportunity to sit in silence for a moment, meditating on my own body, spirit and mind. I was reasonably sure I could make things work in my favor, but that didn't mean that my plan was flawless or without extreme danger. I still needed to figure out how to get the tablet from Dallas into police hands, and then duck the police long enough to get the pieces to fall into place.

"Remember how I said you were an idiot?" Rivkah's voice pulled at me, guiding me out of my meditative state and back into reality and the moment. I took a few moments to allow my eyes to drift open before looking her way and nodding. "You're also insane," she finished—but instead of the fury that had been on her face before, there was only concern. I nodded, unfolding my legs from under me, rising from the floor to check on her work in silence. It was flawless as usual, and I could feel her concern and power in the amulets and trinkets she had prepared for me. It would be less potent than if I had made it, but there was also less chance of a rushed mistake. I nodded.

"Thanks, Rivkah; you did a great job."

"Atah Gabor l'olam Adonai," she muttered, giving the credit for her hard work to HaShem—but I saw her blush at the praise, anyway. Everyone needed those attaboys sometimes.

"Well, thanks to y'all, at least my crazy has a

chance to succeed." I moved to my desk and reached into the middle drawer to retrieve my Jericho 941. Not the most popular choice in firearms, here in the States—but thanks to its design, allowing me to switch calibers with minimal tinkering, it had become my favorite while in the IDF. I checked the clip, ensuring that I wouldn't be surprised when the time came to use it, and after a moment of hesitation grabbed another two boxes of ammo from the drawer. I looked up to see Rivkah's pierced and raised eyebrow. "I said I was going in prepared this time."

"Evidently," she responded, not impressed. She wasn't the sort that enjoyed being around guns, no matter how many times the thing had saved my life. I shrugged and slipped the pistol into its holster under my blazer, and nodded—as much to myself as to Rivkah.

"Okay," I said, feigning a confidence I didn't have. "Out into the world I go."

The phone store had been both more expensive and less complicated than I had been expecting. Once I told them I had lost my phone and needed a new one, they immediately sprang into joyful action. They showed off their latest and most hi-tech toys, assuring me that this one's camera could zoom in to a new microscopic level, and this one played music so clearly you would swear you were sitting in a concert hall. I enjoy gadgets; I do. I continue to be fascinated by all of the technology available, and everything our phones can accomplish—but right now, I just needed a replacement. I jabbed a finger at the nearest smartphone that looked familiar and paid cash for it; I thought it would be faster that way.

Twenty minutes later—after I had signed their contracts, validated services, and transferred all of my old stuff from the cloud—I was out the door with a new, hopefully not-haunted phone. I could no longer go on procrastinating; it was time to get started with the dangerous stuff. I scrolled through my contacts, getting used to the feeling of the new phone case, and made the call to Alex. Within thirty minutes, I was meeting him over by West Campus.

"Thanks for meeting with me, Alex; shalom alechem[55]." He was a huge man, easily standing 6' 7", earning him the nickname Goliath at the synagogue. I was sure he could have become a professional athlete if he had wanted to; what football team wouldn't want a guy who looked like he could eat lead and spit nails?

"Alechem shalom[56], Ze'ev," he responded, eying me suspiciously. I guess I couldn't blame him; he didn't know about the Beit Din, or what I did for a living. As far as he was concerned, I was either in private security or private investigations. All he knew is that I occasionally had useful tips, and an uncanny knack for being at the weirdest crime scenes he had ever seen. I reached into the backpack where I had stuffed all of my essentials, and pulled out the tablet. It was still in a ziplock bag, which in turn was wrapped up in a hand towel.

"You can keep the towel," I offered, as he looked at what I handed him.

---

55 Hebrew greeting "Peace be upon you"

56 The Standard response, "Upon you be peace"

"Fucking shit, Zev; is that blood?"

I winced as he pulled the tablet's baggie out from its hiding place, and nodded.

"Are you kidding me? Whose blood is that, Zev?"

"I don't know her name; it's connected to a crime in Dallas that they need to deal with—just an anonymous source, dropping off some evidence," I suggested.

"That isn't how this works, Zev. You aren't anonymous, and neither am I. When they ask me where I got a piece of evidence connected to an injury . . . " He trailed off, seeing me wince again.

"An assault?"

I shook my head.

"Goddamnit, Ze'ev; if you are seriously handing me something attached to a murder, I will kick your ass so hard that . . . " He sighed. "What the hell am I suppose to do, man? This isn't the movies; I'm going to have to fill out paperwork, and they will grill the shit out of me to find out where I got this. Why do you have it?"

"I was doing some work in Dallas, stumbled on the crime scene, and suddenly gangbangers and cops were everywhere; it was too dangerous to stay, so I ran." That wasn't the biggest lie; hell, it was almost honest. He nodded, buying the story, and sighed; it sounded like the groan of an ancient oak tree. He didn't know everything, but he knew that I sometimes found myself in bad situations.

"Okay. I'll see if I can't cook up a story about this being from an old CI, or something; but seriously, you owe me. You owe me something fierce."

I nodded; it was true, and if I wanted to be able to

continue exploiting this relationship with Alex, I would need to make good on that. I started to turn away when something else occurred to me.

"Hey, do you know a Sargent Zalot?"

"I know him, but not very well. Why?" The look Alex gave me was one of sheer exhaustion; maybe I should deal with this other stuff, and then find a way to inform Alex that at least two members of the Austin Police force were necromantic cultists, bent on raising the dead. One problem at a time. I smiled and shook my head with a shrug.

"Who do we really know these days, right?" I asked in return, before heading to my car—one problem at a time.

A short drive later, I pushed through the doors of Ancient Mysteries once more and looked towards the counter. I swallowed a curse; Becky was behind the counter. Becky was not a fan of mine, which wasn't a surprise; I tended to rub a lot of people the wrong way—especially in this community. She glanced up and scowled when she saw me.

"Look who decided to show up and consort with the witch." Her voice was dry, and devoid of kindness.

"Hello, Becky; is Amanda here?"

"Does it bother you, relying on her help, while at the same time looking down your nose at us?"

I scanned the shelves, more to hide my irritation than because of any embarrassment. "Do I look down on you? I don't think I look down on you."

"Bullshit."

I frowned, looking back at her. I knew where this was coming from; Becky's brother had wanted to study with me, and learn from me. He considered himself a Christian mystic, and a massive fan of Crowley. He had been extremely excited about the idea of a bona-fide "Jewish Magician" joining his inner circle of practitioners. I had tried to decline politely, but the man had been insistent. Finally, it had taken me breaking down exactly why I had no interest in joining his group. He had taken it hard, and Becky had taken it out on me ever since.

"Is Amanda here?" I asked again. Becky may not like me, and she certainly wasn't the person I wanted to see, but I appreciated her honest disdain for me. No false kindness or manners with her. She glared at me for several moments before she jerked her head towards the back hallway. Further into the store were a few rooms, used for meditation and teaching classes. I nodded and stalked past her, ignoring her pointed glare.

Amanda was sitting against a wall on a meditation pillow in one of the back rooms, writing in a small journal; I knocked to let her know I was there. She pulled her eyes from the pages of her writing with some hesitation, and offered me a small, sheepish grin when she saw me.

"Hey, Amanda."

"You need something, don't you, Zev?"

"Giving Tree," I muttered in the way of explanation and was rewarded with a stifled giggle from her.

"Are you going to keep coming back until I'm just a stump?" she asked.

"Never; you're never going to be anything other than a towering pecan." She smiled at that; she was from a little north Texas town with a lot of pecan trees. I knew the imagery would make her happy.

"Okay, what do you need this time? Did you figure out where that knife was from?"

I shook my head, moving into the room and sliding down the wall next to her and onto one of the pillows.

"I'm going to be honest, Amanda—the run-in I had the other day wasn't pleasant, it was dangerous. I'm dealing with some bad stuff right now."

She sat up a little straighter, looking around as though someone might be eavesdropping. "Like when, like, the ghost was . . . "

I nodded. "Like the bhoot, only worse. A lot worse."

I watched her shudder. It had been a pretty harrowing experience for her; at once terrifying and reaffirming. I knew the feeling. I reached up and touched her shoulder, giving it a gentle squeeze. "That's why I'm asking for help; I just—I can't deal with everything on my own, you know?" She nodded slowly. She was a good person, and she would probably have helped me even if she didn't know me. "What do you know about necromancers?"

That got me a look. "That's a big question, Zev; I mean, different people have different ideas of what that means—like some people would call mediums necromancers." That was true; I was one of those people. "Others would say anyone that messes with dead things is, or someone who tries to raise the dead, or just defy death—like, it can be a lot of things."

"The occultist that attacked me was a necromancer, Amanda—the raising-the-dead type." I watched the fear and loathing crawl across her face.

"People can really do that?"

"Some; there's a cost to mind and soul for doing it, but if they are willing to make the figurative and literal sacrifices . . . " I shrugged. "Almost anything is possible, Amanda."

"Okay; so necromancers are real, how can I help? That seems above the burning-sage-and-laying-down-some-crystals pay grade."

I chuckled at that; she wasn't wrong. "Are you still friends with that that Anthony guy?"

She nodded, though I could see the apprehension in her face. She had told me about Anthony in confidence; a very special kid who seemed to be able to tap into the nature of the world, but who had suffered through so many group homes as to be nearly broken. She didn't want to break Anthony's trust, but I knew—just like the giving tree—she wouldn't say no. "Great, I need to talk to him."

Amanda gave him a call, and relayed to me that he would get here as soon as possible; "as quickly as possible" turned out to be three hours later. I was still in that meditation room, pacing back and forth, trying to figure some of the smaller details of my night; I wanted to get as much of this done before the sun set and I became a sitting target for every cultist or ghoul within the city limits. It didn't help that every few minutes Becky walked past the doorway and glared in at me. Just as I was getting ready to give up and leave, a pale young man with bone-white hair peaked his head through the door. His eyes were watery, and so blue as to almost be clear. If not for the eyes, I probably would have thought he was an albino. Prophet, seer, psychic; people had called him a lot of things. He was a recluse, from what I had been able to glean—but I could immediately figure out why. He looked unusual, true; but he also glowed with a hint of the divine. Whatever had given Anthony his gifts had left a mark. If he wasn't careful, he could easily become a cult leader or a victim of fearful men.

"Anthony." It wasn't a question, even though I had never met him in person. He recoiled; it seemed that fear was his constant companion. I scratched the notion that he could be any kind of leader; this kid—and he was a kid, probably no older than 19—was too nervous and terrified to ever lead anybody. He was dressed in ratty torn pants and a dingy t-shirt, and carried a threadbare backpack.

"Yes, sir." His voice was beautiful—the opposite of those things that spoke from beyond the grave; instead it sounded like a clear bell ringing through a crisp autumn morning.

"Great; you want to come in and sit down?"

Step-by-step, Anthony walked into the room, looking around as though someone might be hiding just out of sight to jump him. If I had to guess, he had probably suffered enough under other peoples' fear often to gouge great claw marks through his psyche. I let him take his time, even though I was antsy to get moving. Growing up Jewish in North Texas had given me some hint as to what he had gone through.

"Amanda said you needed help—I don't know what you've heard, but I don't have any, um, powers or anything like that." I wondered if he was being modest, or if he was trying to hide the truth from me.

"I do need help, Anthony, but you don't need to do anything but talk and maybe sit through some prayers." He shot me a look. He wore small silver crucifix around his neck—it almost surprised me; I doubted the church had left the kid unmolested, or had been kind when they discovered him. "Not really a prayer; more like meditation." He still looked suspicious, but at least I was using phrases that he found non-threatening. I gestured to one of the meditation pillows and took a seat myself. Even though he was nervous—maybe even scared—the way he moved was almost hypnotically smooth. I made a note to research this kid, once all this was done; there was no way he was just a gifted human. He could be a changeling, some unwitting sheyd child, or something altogether different. The more I watched him and heard his voice, the more it became obvious that he didn't belong here, with humankind.

"You know about the existence of energy; the supernatural." I observed his face. If he was genuinely religious, I could risk offending him and losing his help. I didn't want that. I was relieved when he gave me a slow nod. "I'm looking for someone that is using that energy to do bad things."

"And you think I can find this person?"

"I know you can, Anthony; you're . . . " How much to say, when even I was mostly in the dark? "You're an empath, you can feel those energies, and with a little bit of direction I think you could help me pinpoint where the bad energy is gathered." I couldn't read his face very well. He seemed to be transitioning between frustration, curiosity, and fear. After several moments he finally spoke.

"What do you know about me?" There it was, he wanted to know what I thought he was, but that was tricky; I didn't actually know very much—I had suspicions, of course.

"Not a lot, Anthony," I shrugged in answer, and I read the disappointment on his face. "But—I do understand that you are different, and that there answers out there. If you help me now, I promise I will do everything in my power to help you discover those answers." I watched him, hope warring with skepticism. He didn't have a lot of trust left in his heart. A lifetime of foster homes and abuse could do that to anyone. After several moments of internal dialog, he nodded.

"Great, thank you." I pulled a map of Texas out of my back pocket and spread it on the floor; I had written several words in Hebrew across the map, as well as notating in English here and there the important places and events involved in this work. As I explained the situation to Anthony in depth, I had to stop several times to attempt to explain metaphysical concepts to him. He was hungry for knowledge. He thought if he had more pieces of the cosmic puzzle he could solve his own enigma. I wish I could tell him it was that easy, but for now I tried to focus his attention on the matter at hand. As we hunched over the map, I walked Anthony through small bits of spellwork and magic—difficult across the language divide. I had never used any sort of magic outside of Hebrew, and he didn't have any knowledge of the language at all. It wouldn't help him to stumble over words, trying to discern intention without understanding, and so we worked in English.

His skin reminded me of the alukah, so pale as to be luminous; his eyes glowed with a gentle light as we begun working with actual magic. But where before my encounter had been with a rotting hag of corruption and decay, Anthony bled life and healing from his pores. He was different also from Domah; his energy and presence were not oppressive, like the mighty aura of the angel—but I suspected it might be related. Research for another time. For now, we had a cult to stop.

CHAPTER XIII

I KNEW WHERE Basken was, in theory. Anthony had been rocky; the newness of trying to harness his natural abilities causing him to stumble—but he *was* a natural, and an intensely curious student. Now I only had to survive long enough to use that information. I stepped out into brisk Autumn night, and gazed up towards the sky. Once upon a time, Austin had been a city where you could see the stars at night. That was a long time ago, now. I wondered how places like Ancient Mysteries would survive, as Austin moved further and further from being weird to being a tech hub. More than that, how long would it be before the Beit Din decided someone better—or more devout—than myself was needed in Texas? For now, I was worrying about nothing, a luxury I certainly didn't have. I drove through town; even as crowded as Austin was getting, it seemed to slow down in the fall, as though no one wanted to face the mediocre chill that November brought with it. That was fine by me; the fewer people who were out and about tonight, the lower the potential for collateral damage. That wasn't something I usually had to consider, but with both ghouls and Basken out for blood, I couldn't take anyone's safety for granted.

Eventually, I pulled off the beaten path to a small cemetery at the southern edge of town. It was the sort of place where those who were sensitive to the supernatural got headaches. Sorrow and pain hung around each small unmarked tombstone, as though they were waiting for some recognition. Buried here—deep under the earth and polite society—were the bodies of confederate era slaves and unknown soldiers. Christians at the time had decided these people didn't deserve respect or the light of God's love, and so consigned them to this forgotten place. I couldn't see any sheydim or dybbukim, but that didn't mean they weren't here. I chose this place because it was the resting place for another kind of entity. Moving through the tall dead grass, I made my way towards the back of the cemetery. I hadn't come here before, and only knew about it from stories that Shanocht had told me. My encounter in Dallas with Mr. Grin had given me an idea—but I still had to figure out a way to put my plan in motion. This place was step one of that plan. Newly-formed ghouls wouldn't have the mental fortitude to tell humans apart, or enough compassion to care. Older things like Mr. Grin might give me a chance to explain, but would likely prefer that we tear each other apart rather than get involved. I reached into my coat and felt the reassuring weight of my pistol.

As I crested a small mound of earth, the rest of the cemetery came into view; as I was expecting, a mass of sickly, slow-moving ghouls—at least twelve of the creatures—milled about, listless and apathetic. There was no food for them here, the flesh and marrow having long since rotted away before the modern age.

These wretched things at the bottom of the hill were exiles. They had been pushed aside by their loathsome kind—confined to a place of death so like those they called home, but without any of the sustenance they craved. They were as condemned as the bones beneath the dark, dry earth here. I'm sure long ago they had tried hunting animals that wandered into their territory, but now, no intelligent thing would venture here. These ghouls were starving; had been starving for years, decades in some cases—but they didn't die. I assume that's part of their punishment, which meant I was about to commit a cardinal sin in the eyes of their kind. I took a deep breath.

In the Talmud, it is taught that if one could see them, no person could endure demons—though whether it is because of their appearance of the sheer amount of them is not terribly clear. But are ghouls demons, created by some power outside of creation? Or were they creations of HaShem? If so, then any hunting of them would be considered cruel, as HaShem had extended full blessings to all of HaShem's creations. It is easy to put all monsters into the "other" column. Ghouls ate bodies, and this forfeited their rights, surely—but I had to consider the existence of hyenas, a creature so similar in appearance and habits to ghouls that it is hard to imagine the two aren't related. Hyenas are certainly a creation of HaShem; even if these wretches were demons by definition, they were still living creatures, of a sort.

On the other hand, was it any better to allow them to exist, in perpetual suffering? Despite the moral arguments on hunting intelligent monsters, I also had to consider my intentions. I was not hunting these creatures to save myself from immediate danger; I was not doing it to ease their suffering. I was doing this because it was a clear and easy way to achieve my ends, and pit ghouls against my enemy—less-than-altruistic motivation, for sure. Moral arguments aside, what I did now was necessary to preserve human life and the sanctity of death.

The only announcement that they were not alone came as I pulled my Jericho from its holster and fired three times. Two ghouls dropped into the dirt, one laying still, the other twitching as its inhuman physiology attempted to shrug off the two large holes that now punctured its torso. The rest of them panicked, trying to dive towards their burrows and nests. I fired again, and a fourth time. The first missed, but the second scored, this time in a knee. Perfect. I moved down the hill toward the injured ghoul. It was grasping its knee, crawling away using its good leg and free hand. The rest of the pack watched me from whatever cover they could find. Even in their weakened state, they could overwhelm me. I projected confidence I didn't feel; not only could these ghouls swarm at any moment—I was still inside Austin city limits, and if civilians were to come by or call the cops, it would be bad for everyone involved. I stopped next to the injured ghoul and raised my voice.

"Your king made an attempt on my life; I know he doesn't care about you, but your lives . . . " I looked down at the ghoul cowering at my feet. Inside, my stomach rolled; I was playing the cruel man, a part that didn't sit with me well. I could tell myself that I would never behave in such a way towards a human—but the creature at my feet could think, reason, and feel. How far could I push my inhumanity before I was no better than a ghoul? " . . . Your lives belong to him."

I pulled the trigger one last time. The lifeless body of the ghoul fell sideways. "Let your king know that the Wolf has good ears, keen eyes . . . " I took a step back, not turning my back to the creatures. " . . . and sharp teeth."

I turned and walked away, deliberately and slowly. To run would give them a clear sign of fear; it would trigger the hunter instinct, and I would be ripped apart before I reached my car. But I could hear them emerging.

But I could hear them emerging. I could hear the sickening sound of tearing flesh and cracking bones. They wasted no time in cannibalizing the corpses of their fallen, even going so far as to rip into the one that was not dead yet; its screamed echoed through the small graveyard, no doubt giving nightmares to any children within earshot. That was three crimes I committed against Baalrachius today: I released three captives from their punishment, I had murdered ghouls, and I had fed his penitent prisoners. Word would get back to Baalrachius or his minions before too long, and I would have very little time to redirect their rage.

From my car, I called Rivkah to keep her updated; and then after a moment of thought, I called Sara, too, to check in. I didn't want her any more worried than she already was. It was a quick call, since she was at work—but just a few moments of talking to her made me miss her warm embrace. Not for the first time, I wondered when I could leave this dangerous life behind. I could maybe get a job teaching. Professor of Jewish studies would be a cushier job, which would involve a lot fewer knife fights and demonic entities. Well, until they came looking for me, anyway. The moon was bright overhead, a false comfort during the night. A little bit of light wouldn't dissuade anyone from taking a shot at me, and until this was all over, I couldn't be safe. There were still a few parts to the puzzle to piece together. Namely, how to get back off the ghoul's kill list when all was said and done. They wouldn't hesitate to kill a human just to be rid of a headache, and I couldn't exactly offer them anything. Without realizing it, Basken had broken my uneasy truce with Shalnacht and made me a target to all of his kind. It was his most effective move. I needed to figure that out as quickly as possible, because after I made my grand play, I wouldn't have time to think of a next step.

I set my phone down on the dash and watched the stars for a moment. This far south of the city proper, you could still see stars. Austin had changed immensely in the last twenty years, going from what amounted to a sleepy hippy town to the next silicon valley. No standing in the path of progress, I suppose. Unless you were talking about magic—that had stopped progressing sometime in the 1600s, and had taken quite a few steps backward. There was only one thing to do now: wait. The timing had to be perfect. I closed my eyes.

There are different forms of meditation; some in which you go entirely into your mind and block out all external stimuli, some in which you became hyper-aware of every moment as it happened, and a handful of other forms. I let a deep breath fill my lungs, whispering a short prayer as I exhaled, and allowed myself to slip into meditation. I focused all of my attention on the sounds around me,

Nights in Texas are never silent; within the bustling cities, there are always cars and construction. The sounds of wheels racing along asphalt create a steady thrum of white noise that can drown out the nuance of the world. I could just pick up that hum in the far distance if I focused my attention on it—but I was listening for something else. Predators succeed because they're able to move nearly silently; but only nearly. Every ounce of my concentration was bent towards identifying predators before they could close in on me. Murphy's Law dictated that something would go wrong; perhaps I wouldn't be able to find Basken, or maybe the ghouls wouldn't take the bait. I found myself wondering how good Basken really was; could he scry at any time? Did he already know that his attack using Marcus had failed? If he had his eyes on me since then during all this planning, it could all be pointless. People are always the unknown factor when it comes to anything like this. Plans fall apart based on human unpredictability. We are messy, messy creatures. My plan relied on several different intelligent, willful people, all doing what I wanted them to do when they had no impetus to play along.

I spread my awareness out, pushing at the limits of what humans can do. My mind was immediately overwhelmed by the presence of life and consciousness all around me. For a moment, all of my thoughts were drowned out by the existence of ants, snakes, and spiders, not to mention billions of bacteria. "Thoughts" is probably too strong a word for what I experienced in that moment. I reasserted my individuality as quickly as I could, the buzz of living things fading into the spreading pool of awareness around me. I hoped I wouldn't have to be in the state for too long; I could already feel the presence of insect minds digging against mine. We aren't supposed to be this connected. It feels about exactly what you expect it would feel like; like they are under my skin. Thousands, maybe millions of insects under my skin at once, scrabbling, gnawing, skittering. While I didn't know of anyone personally, I had studied cases where people had lost their minds to hives and colonies of insects. I often wondered, during those studies, if those people truly lost their minds or if they simply abandoned themselves to join the swarm. The lure of connection is always strong.

I continued to push outward, ignoring the siren call of the hives. Once I had pushed out my consciousness enough, the scratching at my skull eased. The drawl of losing myself was stronger than ever, though. It was a necessary risk; I had no other early warning system. I assumed that Basken was going to be attempting something horrendous and big tonight—at least that's what had come out of my meeting with Anthony. If we were wrong, it would likely mean my death; but I was pretty confident in my source and my plan. I'm not a gambling man, especially when my life is at stake.

I don't know exactly how long I was in this state, aware of everything at once; it could have been minutes or hours. I was so wrapped up in the effort of keeping myself that I almost missed the entire reason I had spread myself so dangerously thin. I had to filter it through the snuffling of coyotes and chirping of the crickets—but underneath it all, long, gangling limbs whose joints clicked as they moved through tunnels. At first, it was just a trickle—easy to miss among the other sounds—but it was growing. More and more clawed feet were scrambling through the earth, towards me. I pulled myself back in, disconnecting from the world around me one inch at a time. It hurts; it feels like bits of my Ruach[57]—my soul—are being left behind; this bit with a family of foxes, this bit on a cactus. But little by little, I find myself only aware of the dark, stifling, stuffy car around me. I turn the keys, letting the sound of the revving motor sing to me for a few moments. My stomach is leaden and sinking, only buoyed by the bubbling sensation of pure fear that I had been suppressing since I had first encountered an armed man in my apartment. I've dealt with the dead before. I've butted heads with cultists, too—but Basken had made himself into something of a nemesis; he was more capable of planning than most of the things I had faced. Then there were the ghouls . . .

I reached into the glove compartment and retrieved my handgun, making sure it was loaded; several talismans rested in my pocket. Basken and Baalrachius. The undead and the eaters of the dead; I was trapped between the two, but in HaShem, I had

---

57 Hebrew meaning "breath" or "soul"

all the strength I needed. I quelled my anxiety again; I would deal with the ulcer when this was over. I planned on waiting a few moments to let them close the distance, when a sudden green light appeared in front of the car. It moved slowly, and with a horrible catch in my throat, I realized what I was looking at. I flipped on the headlights; bright white light flooded the empty roadside in front of me. Empty except for the gaunt form of Mr. Grin, standing calmly, cigarette in hand, smiling wider than anything human-shaped had a right to smile.

"Mother fucker!" Not the best prayer, but all I had at that moment; even as I shouted, I put the car in drive and slammed on the accelerator. Grin calmly stepped back and watched as the car passed; I watched him disappearing in my taillights just long enough to see a dozen or so ghouls swarming from behind him, giving chase.

I was speeding; hell, you would be speeding, too, if a literal army of ghouls was chasing you. I slapped at the overhead light and checked the map on which I had scribbled notes with Anthony earlier. Split-second timing was not the thing at which I was best. I didn't have many options at this point; my original plan had involved calling in the police to do the heavy lifting, but with Grin on my tail, I didn't know if I had time to wait for the police to get involved. Luckily, I was heading north on I-35; the chances of getting pulled over were nearly nil. I glanced in my rear view again. It looked like a clear night on a Texas highway, but occasionally I could see one—darting out of an alleyway, leaping roof-to-roof or riding on the back of one of the big rigs. As soon as I spotted one ghoul, they were gone. These were no young creatures eager for blood. These were hunters and soldiers. I didn't see Grin, but that was hardly comforting; all that meant was that I didn't know where he was. I had hoped that I wouldn't see him again, but my actions must have made him decide that he had made a mistake, sparing me in Dallas. The group had my scent, probably literally. I felt like each time one of the hyena-like monsters let me catch a glimpse, it was closer than before.

I was swerving through traffic, driving dangerously, almost drunk with fear. My lips moved almost under their own power, as the words of prayers of protection and spilled out of me. The red and blue flashing lights behind me pulled me out of my trance, and let me know that it was time for drastic action. My eyes glanced at the map on my dashboard. Five miles. How much havoc did I need to cause to bring everything together?

"Tohu V'bohu[58]," I muttered; mishmash, the chaos of creation. I was there, and with beginningness[59] I aimed out the window and fired over the top of the police cruiser behind me. A big bang would have to be the catalyst that brought this together. I had their attention now; before too long, a second army would be chasing me. I slammed my foot

---

58 A reference to the Bereshit, or Genesis, the "chaos" before the first day.

59 A translation of the beginning of the Torah. "With beginningness"

down, abandoning all pretense of safety. My prayers moved from being for my safety to being for the other people on the road. Any collateral damage that occurred tonight was squarely on my shoulders. Luckily, my exit was just ahead. I hit it at full speed, and nearly launched the car through the air; it was all I could do to control the thing. I ran lights, and sped through the new backroads of urban sprawl towards Elgin. At the speed I was going, it wasn't long before I was close enough to what would amount to a final stand that I needed to think about losing my tails.

I was getting more practice at this than I wanted. I slid through the backroads with the ease of someone who grew up and learned to drive on shitty dirt roads, and as soon as I lost sight of the red and blues for a moment, I killed the lights and slammed on the brakes. My belt was off before the car even finished sliding to a stop. I didn't have time to dawdle; this was it.

CHAPTER XIV

J BARRELED THROUGH the underbrush as quickly as I could. In my hand, I held a small amulet—one of the talismans that Rivkah had painstakingly created for me. It was well-made; she had an eye for the details, and the focus on making it perfect infused her intention deep into the pewter of the amulet. My thumb moved over the grooves in the talisman; 183 angelic names, written so small as to be nearly invisible to the naked eye. The second firmament according to the Sefer HaRazim[60]; as out of breath as I was, as distracted, I intoned each name as carefully as I had just a few nights ago in Memphis—although this time, I paid careful attention to the names of the second order. This was a more meticulous version of the talisman, which I usually wore to help avoid detection. It invoked the names of angels of the morning mists, allowing me to be like mists in the minds of those around me—fleeting and intangible, in theory, anyway. I slipped through the trees; I could hear the sirens behind me. I didn't know how long it would take for the police to find my abandoned car and give chase through the trees. Up ahead, I could make out small fires and the

60 The Book of the Angel Raziel

flickering figures of people through the trees. This was going to work!

Just as I was beginning to think I was a fucking genius, I felt the balled fist connect to the side of my head, sending me sprawling. I landed in a heap at the foot of a large pine tree. My vision was swimming from the impact, but I was thankful that I was still conscious. A few feet away, watching me with disinterest, were Mr. Grin and two of his ghouls. I stood as best I could, my limbs protesting the movement, pain blossoming in my skull with every heartbeat. I raised a hand, intending to explain that the people they really wanted were just over there—but even as I did, one of the ghouls darted forward and caught me by the shoulder. Its talon pushed into my flesh as it lifted me off the ground. I gripped its arm, trying to lift myself off of its claws or at least ease the pressure a little, my legs flailing like a toddler throwing a fit. The grey skin of its face tightened, pulling back in what looked like a feral snarl—but I realized must be a smile. What sort of status would it achieve by bringing me down? It used its free hand to pound several punches into my stomach, before slamming its fist into my face and tossing me away.

I could feel my eye swelling shut. What irony it would be to be killed here and now, mere feet from wrapping up this Basken bullshit. I pushed myself up from the ground. If I could get my gun out from my shoulder holster, I would at least have a fighting chance against the ghouls. My weapon was almost out when the other ghoul—the one who hadn't punched me—moved forward and kicked me with bone-shattering force, sending me flying, the gun falling from my hand and into the brush. Pure agony exploded inside my chest. I wasn't able to take a breath; I gasped and gaped on the ground, watching as Grin and his ghouls emerged from the trees. Then they stopped, looking—almost as one—up and past me.

I rolled onto my side, taking my eyes off the ghouls to see what they were staring at. It was a massive clearing in the middle of these woods; fire pits roared here and there, and people in black robes hovered near each fire. I doubt the ghouls cared much about the rituals—but the altars, and the shambling corpses that moved between the fire pits? They would definitely care about those. Without even the suggestion of a word, Grin inclined his head towards the cultists filling the clearing, and the ghouls rushed past me—vengeance on ragged wings.

With their attention off of me, I pulled myself up; each breath was a monumental struggle, like trying to sip through a broken straw. The pain that accompanied each movement left me with little doubt about how serious my injuries were. There were gunshots, shouted magical incantations, hisses and groans. All around me, Basken's cultists and the ghouls waged their own personal little war. If not for Mr. Grin, I would have probably put the victory squarely on the cultists—but although they outnumbered the corpse eaters, they seemed terrified by the ghouls. It was a little silly, in my opinion. These were people who had decided to raise the dead, who had engaged in murder and horrid rituals. Evidently they hadn't been prepared for there to be other horrifying things hiding in the shadows, other than themselves.

I dragged myself through the battle. My body didn't want to go on; every step was a monstrous effort, but my fatigue wasn't just physical—all around me were atrocities. The cultists had been desecrating and raising the dead. Nearly everywhere I looked were bodies that had been violated. Shambling corpses, with strange and unholy sigils carved into their flesh. They weren't rotting; these had been stolen after embalming. The walking dead fought with the ghouls silently, with no emotion on their faces; puppets that belonged only to the cult. While that was the worst of it, I also had to bear witness to the actions of the ghouls themselves. I had led the ghouls here; what they did to these people was my doing. Even necromancers were still humans—and they were dying, albeit not easily. Between the undead and the knives and drugs of the cultists, the ghouls were losing as quickly as they were taking—but the chaos suited my purposes. As long as their attention was on each other, my talisman would have no problem allowing me to slip through the holes in their focus. I considered turning around and hiding in the woods; letting the cops deal with this mess would be much safer for me in the short run. Just as I turned this idea in my head, I was hit by something intangible and horrid.

My stomach lurched and I buckled over, spilling my lunch onto the ground. I couldn't attribute it to the pain I was in, either; something else was pressing down on me. All around me, magic was being used to animate these corpses and fight the ghouls—but this thing humming through the air and churning my stomach was more powerful and darker than the other magics. This was something decidedly Treif; unholy to its very core. Whatever spell Basken was weaving was going to be devastating not only to everyone and everything here, but to the very soul of creation itself. It had to be stopped.

I could see him on the far side of the meadow. I assumed it was him, anyway—a figure in black robes filigreed with gold runes. He held his hands in the air, and a sickly pale green light was emanating from him. Power came off of him in steady, throbbing waves, visible to the naked eye. My gun was gone, but I still had my knife. I started moving again; skirting through the edge of the battleground, I had no way of knowing when Basken would complete his spell—I only knew I had to reach him before he did. Each step was a battle for me; between the nauseating waves of energy coming off of Basken and the throbbing pain that infused my entire body, I could barely press forward.

I was close enough that I could hear him now; his voice was thin, almost tinny. It matched the voice from the tablet from Dallas, if a bit more strained than before. He sounded a lot less confident now; even still, his words were digging into my flesh like material things. That isn't hyperbole, either; while I didn't recognize the language he was speaking, it was in direct opposition to the language of creation. Things swirled within the words he uttered, existing in those waves of green light that washed over the area where Basken stood. I was close now; close enough that any one of them could finally spot me, if they weren't so intent on their ritual. I watched for a moment as his hands carved intricate runes through the too-heavy air. I slipped my knife into my hand and flipped it open. I considered saying another prayer, or the Sh'ma[61]; after all, the Sh'ma[62] was supposed to be the last thing any Jew said before they died. I wasn't ready to die just yet; I was only prepared to end this.

I stepped forward, directly behind Basken; now I was too close, too out of place—one of his followers saw me and started to shout, but I wasn't going to wait for the bad guy speech or theatrics. I slammed my knife into Basken's hand and ripped down, aiming to sever whatever nerves I could. As soon as my knife was free, I reached my other arm around his throat and kicked the back of his knee, pushing him down. My knife ended pressed against his chest, right above the heart. I grinned wildly at the other men. I had to look somewhat insane; I could taste the blood in my mouth, and was sure it was staining my teeth. I had to nearly shout over Basken's howls of pain, as the spell he had been working faded to nothing. I felt a little insane—but just a little.

"Howdy, Basken; this a good time for a chat?"

Basken was still squirming in my grip, staring at his ruined hand. I wasn't sure if he needed his hands to work magic—but he had been waving it around like maybe it was necessary. Either way, he definitely needed his focus to cast spells, and I had broken that

---

61 "Sh'ma Yisrael, Adonai Eloheiny, Adonai Echad"

62 Hear Israel, Adonai is G-d, G-d is one"

as easily as a piece of matzah[63] on Pesach[64]. The two men that had been standing with Basken started to move closer, but halted when I wiggled the knife against Basken's chest. His howls had finally stopped, although he still struggled.

"Now, now; we're just going to chat—no need to get all bent out of shape. Maybe you should be helping the others." The two men didn't take their eyes off of me; they weren't going anywhere, but that was hardly surprising.

"How did you find me here?" Basken croaked from behind his red mask.

"Well, I know I'm no 'lord of flesh;' but did you think I wouldn't find you?"

"She told me it was safe; that you were nothing, a nuisance to be crushed. You should never have had the power to defy me!"

She? Who the hell was he talking about? I scanned my memory as carefully as I could, with the two men menacing me and Basken squirming like a petulant child in my arms. My mind immediately returned to the witch I had killed in Israel, but that should be impossible. I decided that revealing my ignorance might be a tad premature.

"She lies; you should know that—why would you trust her?"

"She served faithfully, in body, mind, and soul. You were the only thing she asked for in return. Exorcist . . . " Basken looked up at me; I could see eyes behind that mask, human and red-rimmed, they looked—for all the world—weary, and sad. I had to

---

63 Unleavened bread

64 Passover

remind myself that this was a man who had killed several people in an attempt to kill me. "You won't escape what is coming for you. You won't survive."

"He is right." Mr. Grin was suddenly standing there, not more than ten feet away; the two men who seconds ago had been standing there lay crumpled and dead at his feet. I spat a curse and dropped my knife, reaching into my pocket and finding the last trick I had up my sleeve. "This has been fun, don't get me wrong, little Wolf—and I appreciate that you have found the real culprits for me."

"Then you don't need me, do you?" I asked, hoping he would agree—but knowing he wouldn't.

"Ah, I would rather just . . . what is it? 'Two birds, one stone?' You know you have violated our kind, too; it just doesn't do to leave you alive." He took a step forward but paused as I held out my hand, a bundle of talismans hanging from it. It was almost a heady rush, seeing him recoil a moment; at least he thought I could be a threat. "You think you can stop me?"

"Maybe, maybe not; but I took the time toward this little meeting, Mr. Grin. I'm not so careless as to not have an exit strategy."

Under my breath, I whispered words of Hebrew, pushing all of my intentions forward and into the air around me. A soft glow began to spread from the amulets. I heard Basken's swift intake of breath, but it wasn't until the golden light began seeping out of my eyes and mouth, like mist on a cold day, that the ghoul retreated a few steps. Through the pain and the distraction and fear, I still had the talisman of the morning mists around my neck; I still invoked those angels.

"There is no enchantment or spell through which I cannot tear, human."

"No," I admitted. "No, there isn't; but that isn't the question—there is a better question." Grin tilted his elongated, feral head at me, so reminiscent of a hyena with mange. "The proper question, is can you push through my spells, kill the both of us, gather your dead and escape before the police burst into this clearing?"

As if to punctuate my question, the blue and red lights of a cruiser suddenly punctured the clearing, and we could hear shouting. For a moment, it looked like Grin was going to risk it—like he would tear through any spell I cast, rip us limb from limb and then take on the police. Instead, he merely nodded, turned, and walked off, calling in those hateful and whispered words that ghouls call a language. Throughout the clearing, ghouls fled into the shadows of the woods, leaving the cultist to their dead and to the cops that were beginning to appear.

"How did you cast a protection spell so quickly, without me noticing?" Basken sounded in awe at that moment. I wanted him to fear me; I wanted him to know that no matter what power he gathered, I had decades of magical and metaphysical training to trump anything he could ever muster. I almost hated to answer him.

"There was no spell. I was bluffing." I tried to stay standing, to keep Basken subdued until the police reached me—but the adrenaline was wearing off; my body was protesting too much. I felt my body give up, even as the police moved toward us, guns pointed in our direction—and I fell backwards into unconsciousness.

&PILOGUE

J **WOKE UP** handcuffed to a hospital bed. I looked around the room slowly—IV drip, my vitals steadily beeping; everything you expect to see in a hospital room, and also Detective Barman sitting in the corner with his head in his hands. He must have heard me peering around, because he looked up and then moved over to the bed.

"Zev."

"Alex."

"You're in some shit, Zev. You know that, right?"

I tried to chuckle, but I couldn't get that deep of a breath in. He shook his head. "Don't. First, this is serious, Zev; second, you have a collapsed lung, so . . . Try not to be a smartass in a way that makes you laugh at yourself." I smiled a little; at least he was trying to lighten the mood. "The fingerprints from that tablet match the man you stabbed and strangled in the woods, Zev; and, uh, the blood matches a murder victim. Kind of a problem, you know?" I nodded, but he wasn't done. "Also kind of a problem is that you stabbed and strangled a man in the woods."

"The, uh—I got carjacked; I was just trying to fight back, man."

"You got carjacked."

"Would I lie?"

"And then you got free, and—what? We have a lot of dead bodies to account for, Zev; and some bad shit, like gravedigging and . . . " he shuddered. I understood; people didn't deal with witnessing the aftermath of Treif magic. It wouldn't surprise me if the entire force on duty that night needed counseling after seeing the desecrated bodies.

"I think there was a rival group, or something. They showed up just before you guys did . . . started fighting; that's how I got free."

"And then you what? Just started fighting, too?" He seemed skeptical, which was fair; but I had an ace up my sleeve, one that was sort of like a magic spell, really.

"Did you know I served in the Israeli special forces?" I asked him; he nodded slowly. Americans had this weird special-forces-worship-syndrome. It made even the most outlandish tale seem plausible. Of course I had gotten free and turned the tables; hell, I probably could have claimed that I fought the entire group by myself. "I think they were following me, and targeting me for getting that tablet in Dallas, Alex." He nodded again. I was giving him what he needed: a nice bow to tie everything together in a way that made sense. He sighed, and moved to unlock my handcuff.

"Look, there are going to be a lot of questions; you are going to testify and help clear this shit up. But, for now, heal . . . if your girlfriend will allow you to." He gave me a kind smile, and walked out the door, where Sara now stood. She looked furious—like I had made plans to get kidnapped and attacked my crazed cultists—which, of course, I had.

"Ze'ev Moses Kaplan!" How did she do mom-voice so perfectly? "I see you aren't under arrest, and I suppose I should be grateful you aren't some sort of murderer?"

Her question made me question; I had very purposefully led ghouls into that clearing. I was responsible for the deaths that happened last night. I would have to live with that—but I would have to live with it alone; I couldn't tell the Beit Din, Sara or the cops.

"Hi, Sara," I said, doing my best to appear sheepish and unassuming.

"Hi, Sara;' is that all you can say?" She approached the hospital bed like a storm that would break at any second, checking my vitals and the equipment to which I was hooked up. "I have to find out you're here from the police, and then watch the news and see all of that . . . How did you survive Ze'ev?"

I shrugged a little, wincing at the excruciating pain it brought. Her face didn't soften any at my pain, but she sighed. "You are so strong; it's going to take more than some crazy cult to take you down." She moved a dial, and suddenly my pain was floating away from me. Actually, I was the one floating away. I could feel my consciousness slipping into morphine dreams. I watched Sara; her face, annoyed and cold, became hazy and dreamlike as I once again relinquished my hold on the waking world.

I stayed in the hospital for a few days; Sara didn't bother coming back, still angry that I had gotten mixed up in something so dangerous—but Rivkah came and spent a few hours with me each day; to play chess, chat and to bring me food that was actually edible.

"You are an insane idiot," she said on the first day, while setting up the board.

"But it did work, didn't it?"

"Just because you survived, and aren't dead yet, does not mean it was a good plan," she shot back.

"Ah; but for some reason, my erstwhile apprentice didn't have a better plan—almost like, it was the best plan I had." I grinned at her from around my burrito. She nodded at me, looking at me with a mix of pity and affection. "Look, I know it was a bad idea, but, what we did was necessary; Basken was doing true evil—not just different magic, not just against our ideas of good and bad, but true evil."

She nodded; I think she was convinced. But even if she wasn't, I was grateful for the company.

When I was discharged from the hospital, Sara was working and Rivkah was meeting with the Beit Din, meaning I had to get an Uber home since my car was still locked up in police impound. I was happy to get home to my little safe place; and really, I was glad to be alone. My time in the hospital had been a constant stream of Sara being not-so-passively aggressive through text message, police questioning and morphine dreams; now I could rest, meditate and pray—all the things I was looking forward to. The hundred or so emails I had received from Nathan Schulman would wait.

I stepped through the door and walked in the darkness towards my bedroom when I realized I wasn't alone. The smell of stagnant rot filled my nostrils; I discounted the idea it was another zombie from Basken—I had ruined his spell casting days with that knife wound, and the dry rot smell was pretty iconic of someone else who wanted me dead.

"I think we can leave the light off, don't you, little Wolf?"

I nodded, my eyes scanning the darkness of my apartment, searching for the shape of Mr. Grin. "Here to kill me?"

"No; I thought about it, I am very tempted by it, but no." The creature in the darkness of my home sighed and shifted. "You are clever—surprisingly clever—and while my master has asked for your death, I think it would serve me better to keep you alive; alive, and with the knowledge that I can find you whenever and wherever I choose."

"You want to use me?" I asked.

"I am going to use you," he clarified. "There is no want here. There is what will happen, and what will happen if you try to refuse me. Because, little Wolf, unlike me, you have people you care about. Unlike my king, I do not discount humanity. I understand what family means to your kind." I nodded to the darkness; I understood the threat. I waited for several moments for him to make some demand before I realized I was alone.

I turned on the light—confirming he was gone and that my belongings were, for the most part, unmolested—before walking to the phone and dialing. I would have to deal with Grin and Nathan, Sara and the police soon, but for now . . .

"This is Milano's Pizza, can I take your order?"

"Hey, it's Ze'ev; just my usual, Tom." For now, I could rest.

About the Author

John never thought he would write horror or darker fiction, he was planning on writing fantasy. But something about setting all of the occult and fantastical elements of fantasy just behind the backdrop of the modern world appealed to him, and he wanted to introduce the world to the incredible mythology of mythic Judaism. He spends his time squirreled away fervently working on the next book or engaging in the 'Obliterate the Globe' project, only taking breaks to record episodes of Madness Heart Radio and Wandering Monster, or to eat, or to play with puppies. John lives with his patient and gorgeous wife Desiree, and maniacal and powerful daughter Aziza. You can find him and the project at www.KaijuPoet.com